BETWEEN THE WATERS

Nan Maynard

Chivers Press • G.K. Hall & Co.
Bath, England Thorndike, Maine USA

This Large Print edition is published by Chivers Press, England, and by G.K. Hall & Co., USA.

Published in 1998 in the U.K. by arrangement with Robert Hale Ltd.

Published in 1998 in the U.S. by arrangement with Robert Hale Limited.

U.K. Hardcover ISBN 0–7540–3417–8 (Chivers Large Print)
U.K. Softcover ISBN 0–7540–3418–6 (Camden Large Print)
U.S. Softcover ISBN 0–7838–0247–1 (Nightingale Series Edition)

The text of this Large Print edition is unabridged.
Other aspects of the book may vary from the original edition.

Set in 16 pt. New Times Roman.

Printed in Great Britain on acid-free paper.

British Library Cataloguing in Publication Data available

Library of Congress Cataloging-in-Publication Data

Maynard, Nan.
      Between the waters / Nan Maynard.
         p. cm.
     ISBN 0–7838–0247–1 (lg. print : sc : alk. paper)
     1. Large type books.   I. Title.
     [PR6063.A889B48   1998]
     823'.914—dc21   98–23164

GW 11998733

*This book is for
John and Tina Burge
with my love*

Author's Note

The old wives' tales tell us that the area between the sea and the canal is spooked with evil. Lovers betray each other; the old and lonely don't live—they just exist, in a welter of memories and self-pity; and the young lose their illusions far too quickly.

Nan Maynard

CHAPTER ONE

February is a horrid little month, furtively nudging the promise of spring whilst, at the same time, hanging on to the coat tails of winter, bathing the world in soft yellow sunshine one day and, the next day, spitting out snowflakes from darkened skies.

Just like my life has been, she thought, bright one day, dark the next, and all because of one man. He can lift me up and throw me down, but he's done it for the last time. Trust betrayed is trust destroyed. There can be no more peace of mind, no relaxation and life together becomes impossible. Tonight she would tell him and it would break her heart to part from him but, for both of them, it would be the only solution.

As she removed the last of her dresses from the huge wardrobe she remembered her grandmother who, in her heyday, had been betrayed by *her* husband. Gran had taken it in her stride, as she had all family problems over the years. Annabel had vivid memories of Gran sitting in her favourite armchair, surrounded by sympathetic relatives. She had still been in her prime then, vital and attractive.

Annabel remembered Gran putting her hands together as if in prayer as she quoted softly, '"Man is born unto trouble as the sparks fly upward". That comes from the book of Job.

1

He was a wise old feller, that Job.'

And Annabel's mum, not to be outdone by Gran, had said sourly, 'Yeh, like the Yiddish proverb "Man macht and God lacht". That means "Man plans and God laughs".'

Gran had given Mum what Annabel called Gran's snooty look which belittled Mum and her habit of showing off whenever she had the chance—she always had to dominate the conversation. Gran sneered about Mum's professed knowledge. 'She's just got a good memory,' Gran said. 'And that's given to her as compensation because she hasn't got a good brain.'

No one was allowed to upstage Gran and steal her thunder.

I guess I'm like her, Annabel mused, I've got to be the tops. I can't take second place—that's why I'm not prepared to overlook this latest infidelity of Alex.

This was the ultimate betrayal—an affair with the girl who owned the Priory Antiques shop in Copmarsh—young, brash and beautiful. No way could Annabel ignore her husband's blatant affair and still hold her head high. Divorce would give her one crowning victory: she was certain that, when the divorce was finalized, Alex wouldn't marry the girl and she would be left, Annabel thought with grim pleasure, crying into her antique vases, the object of pity in the small town which watched the machinations of its residents with genteel amusement. I love Alex, but now I'm going to leave him and I'm going to have some fun. I don't care who gets hurt, just so long as it isn't me. It'll be good to be on the winning team for a change, to gloat over the tears of other women and forget that I was ever stupid enough to cry over a man. This little town which has seen my humiliation can now watch my triumph and I don't give a damn what they say about me. Anything is better than pity.

One bright spot in the wreckage of her marriage was the fact that she was not short of money. Her grandmother had left the bulk of her fortune (from her late husband's brewery businesses) equally between Annabel and her sister, Jessie. Whereas Jess had placed her money into the control of her husband, Albert, Annabel had kept her fortune in her own name. In fact, Alex had never been interested in his wife's money. He had been born into money from the prestigious family estate agent's business and there had never been any financial problems in his life.

At least there won't be any bitter money-wrangling Annabel thought, the divorce should be quick and easy. She bundled the dresses together and threw them on the bed. Then she sat down beside them and wept.

*   *   *

She found a vacant flat in a small white block of

six in a long quiet road between the sea and the canal. She was aware of the local superstition that the area between the sea and the canal was spooked with evil. No one seemed to know how the legend had started, but most of the local people believed it. Annabel's sister, Jess, told her, 'You can't live there, Annabel, it's said to be fraught with evil,' but Annabel laughed and said, 'I could do with a bit of evil for a change. I've had enough of respectability and obeying the rules.'

Jess pursed her thin lips. 'I don't like to hear that kind of talk, Annabel. Two wrongs don't make a right, you know.' 'Oh Gawd, Jess,' Annabel said. 'You sound just like Mum, trotting out the old platitudes; you'll be telling me "A stitch in time saves nine" next, and don't forget, "As ye sow so shall ye reap". Mum had a saying for every situation and they're all daft as far as I can see.'

'You can mock, Annabel,' said Jessie wisely, 'but they're all very true, you know. If you live by them, you won't go far wrong in life.'

'Well, I'd like to go wrong in life just for a change,' said Annabel. 'I'm sick of being Mrs Goody Two-Shoes.'

'And to hell with the people you'll be hurting in this stupid crusade of yours I suppose.'

Don't worry, Jess, Annabel thought, your deadly dull Albert will be quite safe. I wouldn't touch dear Albert with a ten-foot barge-pole.

The two sisters were sitting in a café on the

4

sea front, details of the flat in Romney Place spread out on the table before them.

Jessie, four years older than Annabel, looked quite ten years older. Jessie looked neat and frumpy. She was plump with short fat legs. It was hard to believe that Annabel came from the same stable. She was tall and willowy and her high cheekbones ensured beauty that wouldn't quickly fade. The clothes didn't make the woman, the woman made the clothes, and Annabel chose her clothes well, mostly plain, but obviously expensive. She looked down at the estate agent's note.

'It's a pretty name, Romney Place, don't you think so, Jess? Before the land was reclaimed and built on, it was marshland used by the smugglers years ago to get across to the inn and the rectory to sell their loot.'

Jessie sniffed her disapproval. She had no time for tales of the old smugglers. And, as an ardent church-goer, she rejected the yarns about bygone vicars who had profited from the smuggling. Her husband, Albert, was in the church choir and he, too, hated stories of the olden-time clergy being in cahoots with the smugglers. Malicious folk-lore, he called it, a slur on the church. Albert Freeman had never approved of his sister-in-law's marriage to the glamorous Alex Clifton, the wealthy estate agent whose head office was in the West End of London, a large firm well known in the south of England. Albert had inherited *his* family

5

drapery business in the small town of Copmarsh and was acknowledged as the most prosperous trader in the town. The name, Freeman & Son, was still on the large shopfront although, at this present time, there was no son. Albert and Jessie were childless. The vast, old-fashioned shop was like something in a Dickens novel and Albert was proud of its sprawling departments overflowing into each other. If you turned round in the hosiery section you were immediately confronted by rolls of curtain fabrics. Albert regarded this as a boost to sales.

'Let the customers see all the stuff,' he said. 'They might not realize they need new curtains until they see the materials displayed.'

Then they could turn round from the curtains to an assortment of attractive tea towels and pillow slips which made very nice Christmas gifts. Albert decreed that if there were separate enclosed departments for each kind of merchandise customers wouldn't take the trouble to roam around the store. Whereas if they were confronted by the goods, it could result in sales, which obviously it did. Freeman & Son was an institution in Copmarsh, as everlasting as the war memorial in the town square erected for the fallen in the First World War of 1914–1918.

Albert, now the sole proprietor of Freeman & Son, drove to work daily in a sedate Daimler, whilst Alex Clifton, Annabel's husband, roared to London each day in his Porsche to the glamorous chrome and cream offices where he sold up-market properties to up-market clients.

Alexander Clifton had gone into his father's thriving firm of Clifton, Parry, straight from university. He had very little flair for the commercial side of the old-established firm, but was a decided asset when dealing with clients by virtue of his outstanding good looks, his impeccable manners and general charisma. Alex was a great hit with female clients and if he occasionally mixed business with pleasure he was always discreet. Profit for his firm was always a top priority with him. His parents had died together in a plane crash in India when Alex was twenty-six; and he had stayed on in the large family home in the small Kentish town of Copmarsh, looked after by a housekeeper-cook and her husband—general handyman-cum-gardener.

Alex had met the lovely Annabel Stanton at a barbecue laid on by a local solicitor and his wife. Until that time Alex had written off the local female talent as a no-go area and reserved his philanderings for the more sophisticated women on the London scene, but the lovely, rather aloof, Annabel Stanton had immediately captured his interest. Like himself, she had lost both her parents and, since her sister's marriage, had lived in the family home with just a housekeeper for company. Although she hadn't needed to work after the death of her parents, she had been helping in a local exclusive gown shop owned by one of her old school friends.

Alex Clifton was inundated with invitations to local social events, but seldom accepted them. On this occasion, however, he was at a loose end and decided to pass away an hour or so on the home scene. He was completely bowled over by the lovely, remote Annabel Stanton, particularly as she seemed at first to have little interest in him. That piqued him and made him more than ever determined to make an impression on her.

His subsequent pursuit of Annabel was looked on with much disfavour by Jessie and Albert, dull, respectable Albert, chairman of the local Chamber of Commerce, head chorister at the local church and an eminent resident of tiny Copmarsh perched on the edge of the marshes. Albert Freeman and Alexander Clifton had nothing at all in common. Albert was staid and humourless, whereas Alex was an acknowledged playboy. Albert very reluctantly consented to give Annabel away at her marriage to Alex, and her frumpy sister was her matron of honour. It wasn't the kind of wedding Alex had wanted, but Annabel insisted on being married in the small town, inviting local people instead of the smart set in which Alex had mixed before meeting her.

'We shall live in Copmarsh,' she had insisted, 'and, therefore, we should cultivate a circle of

8

friends locally. Besides which, it will be a welcome change for you after the razzmatazz of the London scene which is, after all, an essential part of your work. You'll find it a welcome change to relax with the locals.'

But Alex had never found it relaxing. He hated the boring locals and their petty problems—protests against proposed motorways, demonstrations against the felling of trees and the like. He had never at heart been a countryman and he cared nothing for the environment just as long as the value of his elegant house was not threatened. Politely he rejected all offers of a seat on local committees and his only involvement with the town in which he lived was his membership of the local golf club where he met the pretty, saucy Rosemary Wharton, a comparative newcomer to the district and his latest paramour. His other affairs had been with women on his London scene and although Annabel had lived for a long time with her suspicions, she had no real basis for accusing him of infidelity. Rosemary Wharton was a very different matter. Their affair was flaunted in front of the town and now Annabel could not ignore it.

Jessie toyed with her toasted teacake. She hadn't wanted to come into this small sea-front café frequented mostly by whom she disdainfully called 'trippers'.

'Let's go back to my place for coffee,' she'd suggested to Annabel, but Annabel had said,

9

'No. Let's go in here and pretend to be holiday-makers.'

Jessie had no desire to pretend to be a holiday-maker in her own home town.

'You can never be sure that these places are hygienic.'

But Annabel laughed. 'Of course they are, Jess. Haven't you heard about trading standards or whatever it is they do about hygiene these days?' She topped up their coffee cups from the silver-plated jug and added cream.

'Divorce is so sordid,' Jessie said.

'I can't think of any other way to rid myself of an unfaithful husband,' Annabel said with a flippancy she was far from feeling, 'unless, of course, I murder him or commit suicide.'

'I wouldn't think you'd feel like laughing about it,' said Jessie sourly.

Annabel's eyes clouded. 'If I didn't laugh, I might cry, Jess, and I'd hate to give him that satisfaction.'

'You should never have married him in the first place. If Mumma and Daddy had been alive . . .'

'If Mumma had been alive,' Annabel cut in, 'she'd have approved my marrying Alex. You know what a snob Mumma was and, after all, the Cliftons were considered to be the local gentry.'

Jessie was momentarily silent. She knew that Mumma would never have approved of her own choice of Albert Freeman if Albert's business hadn't been such a respected and prosperous local institution. Secretly she was glad that Mumma had died before Annabel's marriage to Alex Clifton. She could just imagine how Mumma would have rubbed in the fact that Annabel was marrying 'class', whereas Jessie had settled for 'trade'. However, one thing Jessie was sure of and that was that Mumma would have disapproved of Annabel filing for divorce. No one in the family had ever been involved in divorce proceedings. People overlooked and endured and friends respected that reticence; Jessie hated to think what effect the actions of her rebellious sister would have on her own and Albert's good names.

'I hope you'll be as discreet as possible,' she said, sipping her coffee as if it were poison.

Annabel laughed. 'As discreet as Alex has been? Naturally.'

'You realize of course,' said Jessie stiffly, 'that the scandal will affect Albert's integrity in the town.'

'What on earth are you talking about?'

'I'm just saying that, as a respected local businessman, Albert . . .'

Annabel cut in on her. 'What utter rot!' She gave a curt laugh. 'What has my divorce got to do with Albert?'

'People look up to Albert as a pillar of decency.'

'Well, I'm not going to cite you as co-

11

respondent or tell people I'm having an affair with your precious Albert.'

Jessie was angry now. 'Don't be ridiculous Annabel. It's just that you know how people in small towns talk.'

'Maybe I'd better move to save you embarrassment.'

Jessie was startled. She hadn't envisaged her sister ever leaving Copmarsh.

Annabel looked out of the window at the winter sea. There was nothing else to see, no boats, no swimmers. It's dead, she thought, just like my marriage.

'I shan't make any claim on Alex about the house,' she told Jessie. 'After all, it was his parents' home, never really my home, and I still have half of the money we got for *our* family home when Mumma died, enough to buy a new property. And, like you, Jess, thanks to Daddy and Mumma, I'm not exactly a pauper. In fact, I'm what they might call "a woman of means".'

Jessie shuddered. 'I don't know how you can talk about money at a time like this.'

'I've got to be practical, Jess, and I'd hate to have to ask Alex for money. I'm lucky in that respect.'

Jess put her hands on the table and leant towards her sister.

'Don't you think, Annabel, that if you ignored this latest affair with Rosemary Wharton, it would fizzle out? After all, the slut's had her name linked with other married men in the past *and* she's still single.'

'Maybe she hasn't found one she wanted to marry yet,' said Annabel flippantly. 'You must admit that Alex is definitely what they call "a good catch", not to mention the fact that he looks like the male lead in a sizzling Hollywood drama.'

'And will you be prepared to watch her marry him and move in to your beautiful house?'

'I shan't be watching. I shall be too busy living my own life the way I want to, for a change.'

'Meaning?'

'I told you, Jess. Fun. No holds barred. No more promises of eternal fidelity, no restrictions.'

Jessie was openly shuddering.

'And bring disgrace on the family?'

Annabel shrugged. 'There isn't any family left, except you and Albert, and it isn't any concern of yours. Anyhow, Alex didn't worry about bringing disgrace on the family when he started getting into young Rosemary's frilly panties.'

Jessie flinched. 'Don't be disgusting, Annabel. I don't know what's come over you these days.'

'Rejection,' said Annabel bleakly, her flippancy momentarily gone. 'Rejection, and that's hard to take, Jess, but I'm damned if I'm going to let him see how much I care.'

Jessie wiped her fingers on the tiny paper

13

serviette, rolled it up and put it into an ashtray.

'Well, I must be going, Annabel. I have the WI members coming round later to discuss the summer outings for the orphans from St Bede's. Do you want a lift home?'

'No thanks, Jess, I'll walk. I haven't walked along the sea front for ages. It'll do me good. Remember, we used to do it when we were kids, after church?'

There was a softer look in Jessie's eyes now as she looked at her sister.

'Remember, I'm always here for you if you want anything Annie, you know that.'

Annabel was touched. It was ages since Jess had called her Annie. She smiled at her elder sister.

'I know, Jess dear, thanks, but I'll be OK. Leave the bill, I'll settle it.'

And, as Jessie moved towards the door, Annabel called out, 'Love to Albert.'

Jessie smiled bleakly as she left the café.

CHAPTER TWO

Albert Freeman sat in his small glassed-in office at the top of a short flight of six wide stairs. From this vantage point he could see almost all the ground floor of his large prestigious store, Freeman & Son. Above was a vast loft covering the whole of the building.

This was where all the new stock was stacked waiting for the appropriate time to move it down into the sales departments. Albert was very pleased with his choice of spring stock this year. There were one or two new lines being introduced which he hoped would sell well. He had to admit reluctantly that the little town of Copmarsh was changing. People were looking for more trendy wares. Albert hated the word. He wondered what his grandfather would think if he could see his beloved store now with its drab clothes in the Ladies' Department, and the pretty, frivolous duvet covers in Bedlinen. Albert would not use duvets on his bed. 'What's wrong with sheets and blankets?' he'd said to Jessie once when she had told him that Alex and Annabel were using these duvets. 'Just a big sales con; it won't last. Those things will never replace good old-fashioned blankets.'

Albert derived little joy these days in the section displaying ladies' clothes. Gone were the pretty woollen dresses and winter suits of old. Now there were jeans and garments called by the unglamorous names of sweat shirts and tops. In Albert's opinion these sexless garments made it difficult to differentiate between working-class women and females of the upper social strata and were a disastrous class-leveller. Sweaters with stupid slogans on the fronts and leg-hugging denim jeans held no allure for Albert. He liked feminine women

15

and although Jessie didn't have the flair of her sister, at least she always wore conventional clothes, expensive if not all that spectacular.

Albert rose from his stool and surveyed the shop below. He did this at frequent intervals as it gave him a great glow of satisfaction to survey his little kingdom. Laura Collins, moving from Fabrics to Corsetry, looked up and flashed him a faint, respectful smile. He lifted a hand in salute. It occurred to him suddenly that Miss Collins, as she was called in the shop, was looking a little sad today. He realized then that he had never really noticed her before or appreciated the quiet dignity of the woman. She was part of the fixtures, having started work in the store in his father's time when she was just sixteen. Young saleswomen had come and gone over the years, but Miss Collins remained the same, always helpful, always polite, now promoted to manageress with appropriate modest rises in wages from time to time. She was taken for granted, Albert thought, like the stout timber pillars on the ground floor which supported the building. Albert knew that Miss Collins wasn't really a 'miss'. He had been told that she was a married woman who lived with her aged mother and, vaguely, he remembered hearing that she had a son who was away at school. He had never heard any mention of a husband. Albert watched her as she moved gracefully to hand something to a young girl behind the corsetry counter. The girl nodded and took the proffered docket and, as Miss Collins turned away, Albert noticed again her rather sad face. This time as she passed under his window she didn't look up and quickly disappeared into Fabrics which section was her chief domain and in which she had a small desk and chair in a corner.

Albert sat down again and resumed his paperwork, all thoughts of Miss Collins dismissed. He told himself he was a lucky man to have an empire like Freeman & Son and a quiet, loyal wife like Jessie. Jessie Stanton had been such a suitable match for him. As head of Sunday school she had been a prominent young resident of the quiet little town of Copmarsh, but there had never been any adverse talk abut her. Albert had been her only sweetheart, having started to court her just after the death of his one remaining relative—his father. His father had often talked of the Stanton sisters and their financial status emanating from the family brewery businesses no longer in existence, but which had provided the Stanton family with modest wealth.

At 5.30 Albert checked his gold pocket-watch with the big clock downstairs. Then he stacked the papers on which he had been working into his desk and put the key in his pocket. Downstairs in the store staff were putting covers over some of the goods and preparing to depart. Albert made it a rule to be the last person off the premises, although Miss Collins had a duplicate set of keys. He watched as lights were switched off downstairs and members of the staff left the building. Miss Collins was always the last one to leave and always she made sure that he was downstairs to check that everyone had left the premises before she, herself, left. Then he would lock up in spite of the fact that she had her own set of keys.

Tonight he waited for her customary signal telling him that she was departing and that he was the only one left. This formula had been in operation as long as he could remember. Tonight, however, when she had seen the last employee off the premises, she locked the front door with one of her own set of keys and turned to look up at his office. He went to the door and called down to her, 'Something wrong, Miss Collins?'

'Not really, sir. May I have a quick word?'

'Certainly Miss Collins. Come up.'

'I've locked the front door, sir.'

As she came up the stairs and into his office he drew forward a chair for her.

'Sit down Miss Collins. What can I do for you? Staff problems?'

She sat down awkwardly and twisted her hands together after putting her keys on the desk before her.

'I wondered, sir, if you'd mind me working a little late tonight to get my stock figures up to

18

date. The auditors want them by next week. Normally I could have managed it in the next few days, but I have to ask you, sir . . .' She stopped and interlaced her fingers nervously.

Clearly the woman was distressed. Albert spoke softly. 'Yes Miss Collins. You were going to ask me . . .'

She looked at him squarely and her eyes were troubled.

'If I could have the next three days off, sir. I realize it will have to be deducted from my annual leave. I'm not asking for unpaid leave. There are no sales on now and it's just that . . .'

Her voice trailed off. Albert was surprised. It was so unlike Miss Collins to make waves. Occasionally there were problems with other members of staff proffering feeble excuses for absenteeism, but usually Miss Collins was able to straighten things out without seeking his assistance. Now it was her turn to ask for leniency and it was obviously distressing her.

'I realize, sir, that it's very inconvenient having members of staff creating problems for you and I wouldn't have dreamed of doing it if it hadn't . . .' She stopped, then suddenly she blurted out, 'The thing is, my boy's in trouble at school and I have to go to try to sort it out if I can.'

She looked so stricken that Albert wanted to reach out and gather her to him like he would a child. Instead he said quietly, 'Would you care to tell me about it, Laura?'

19

She was startled at his use of her first name. He was surprised himself. Somehow she had ceased to be Miss Collins and, instead, was a poor young thing in need of comfort. Almost like a daughter, he thought. Then she spoke.

'I'm too ashamed to talk of it, sir ... Mr Freeman.'

She looked at him with desolate eyes. He turned away and got up from his chair. He reached up to a small cupboard above his desk and opened the door. Taking a bottle of sherry from the cupboard he turned to her with a smile.

'A little drink will relax you, Laura. Then you can tell me all about it.'

Without waiting for her reply, he took down two glasses and poured the drinks. Still twisting her fingers she said nervously, 'I shouldn't be wasting your valuable time, Mr Freeman.'

She unlaced her fingers as he handed her the glass of sherry.

'You're not wasting my time, my dear. My employees' troubles are *my* troubles.' He smiled at her. 'Not teetotal, are you?' She smiled back at him—a feeble effort.

'No sir. It's very kind of you.'

'Not at all.' Albert tasted his sherry. Laura sipped hers and threw him a wavering smile. 'This is so good of you, sir.'

'Nonsense. Now, tell me all about it and maybe I can help. Take your time; I'm in no hurry.'

In fact, he had told Jessie he was staying on at the shop for a while tonight to clear up some paperwork, so she was holding dinner back an hour.

'How old is your son, Laura?'

'Fourteen sir.'

'Ah, yes. I've probably been told, but I've forgotten. What is his name?'

'Noel, sir. He was born on Christmas Eve.'

They smiled at each other and he thought, she's really rather pretty. I'm surprised I haven't noticed it before. He wondered if there was a man in her life.

'Before you start, Miss Collins, Laura, put your mind at rest. The auditors can wait, so I don't want you to worry about work.' He smiled gently. 'In fact, I'm a little behind with my own work so I was going to put them off anyway.' It was a lie but he thought it justified.

She took another sip of her sherry and smiled at him.

'You're very kind, Mr Freeman.'

He flexed his hands together after he had taken another good sip of his sherry.

'Well, if we can't help each other, it's a sorry old world.'

He felt a faint rumbling in his stomach and it occurred to him that it would have been nice if he could have taken Miss Collins out for a little meal somewhere, where they could relax and talk but, of course, it was impossible. Jess was expecting him home to dinner and if he were seen with Miss Collins in a public place there would certainly be talk; he was a well-known and well-respected figure in Copmarsh and people in small towns were so narrow-minded. So mused the respectable Albert, pillar of the church, surprised at this new feeling riding him. Was it guilt? Nonsense, he had nothing to feel guilty about, yet why was he feeling like a schoolboy caught with his fingers in the jam? He downed his sherry and felt the liquid burning. He knew that drinking on an empty stomach was foolish, nevertheless, he said, 'Drink up, Laura, and let me give you a refill.' With a little chuckle he added, 'Bird can't fly on one wing, you know.'

Her smile was not so sad this time. In fact, she gave a subdued giggle as she drained her glass, gulping a little as she did so.

Albert got up to refill their glasses. With his back to her he said, 'Tell me what the trouble is, Laura. Maybe I can help.'

This time when he handed her the sherry she seemed a little more at ease. Her fingers lovingly cradled the stem of the glass.

'Drugs, Mr Freeman. He's been accused of taking drugs himself and selling them to other boys.'

She took a good swallow of her sherry as if to brace herself. 'I'm so ashamed, Mr Freeman, you don't know . . .'

Albert put his glass down and, reaching forward, lightly touched her hand.

'It's not your fault, my dear. The fault lies with the school surely. Which school is it?'

'St Crispin's.'

Albert was surprised. It was a very expensive school. How on earth could she afford it?

As if sensing his question she said quickly, 'My ex-husband pays for his schooling. I'd never have been able to afford a school like that.'

'I see.'

Albert was silent, thinking. Then he said, 'You say ex-husband. Are you divorced?'

She nodded. 'Yes, we divorced when Noel was four years old.' She smiled ruefully. 'We had nothing in common really. It was a youthful infatuation for both of us. Clive came from a rich family. We met on holiday in France. We were young and very foolish. I knew it wouldn't last when he refused to let me meet his family. Over all these years he's never wanted to see Noel. He just pays all Noel's expenses, his schooling, his clothing, his holidays, those are usually at camps with the Scouts or naval cadets. My ex-husband's father was a naval captain, but I never met him or his wife.'

'But doesn't your ex-husband make you an allowance?'

She lifted her head proudly. 'No. He has a son and daughter by his present marriage.'

'Does he live locally?'

'No. He lives in Scotland.'

23

'So you never hear from him.'

'No. All Noel's expenses are dealt with by solicitors. I haven't heard from Noel's father at all since our divorce. The solicitors told me about his remarriage and his children.' She raised her head. 'I prefer it this way. Our marriage was a ghastly mistake. I have my mother and I have my son.' Her voice trembled. 'At least, I *thought* I had my son and knew him, but it seems I've failed in some way.'

Albert lifted her hand and patted it.

'You haven't failed, Laura. You're a good, hard-working . . .' he had been going to say 'woman', instead he said, 'girl. You have your pride and so you should, you lead a useful, respectable life and you look after your mother. The blame is entirely with the school and your ex-husband.'

She looked surprised.

'Edward? But he never sees Noel, so how can it be his fault?'

'A boy needs a father.'

As he spoke the words Albert thought, why am I saying this? There is no one needing *me*. The only person who really needs me is Jessie, and now, perhaps, this unfortunate young woman.

The second sherry appeared to have given Laura courage to speak freely.

'Although I do all I can for Noel, I think that maybe he resents me, blames me probably for the breakdown of my marriage, but every time

I try to talk to him about it, he stops me, saying it's not his business. The fact that he has everything he needs doesn't seem important to him. The solicitors acting for my ex-husband make sure that everything Noel has is always of the highest quality, and he has been assured by them that he will receive first-class training for the career of his choice when the time comes.'

'And that is?' prompted Albert gently.

She shook her head.

'He can't seem to make up his mind. He veers from architecture to owning a restaurant. It seems to be a huge joke to him and now . . .' She spread out her hands in a helpless gesture. 'And now, with this awful drugs thing hanging over him . . . I can't understand how he can have connections with drug dealers.'

'Oh, I guess that's easy enough,' said Albert. 'These evil men do their homework, they . . .'

Her agitation got the better of her and she interrupted him.

'If only he had a father to deal with this problem.'

Surprising himself, Albert said, 'Would you like me to go with you tomorrow?'

Laura was surprised too.

'It's very good of you, Mr Freeman, but I couldn't possibly involve you. I'm very grateful, but I'd rather try to deal with it on my own.'

Albert was relieved. He was surprised at himself for offering. It would have been difficult to explain it to Jessie. Also, he was

25

never absent from the store except for annual holidays, and very rare spells of ill health. People would certainly talk.

'Well, you know best Laura, but I'm always available if you want any advice or even if you just need to unburden yourself. It's good to have a sympathetic listener.' He attempted jocularity. 'I could do with one myself on occasion.'

She smiled at him. 'I can't believe that, Mr Feeeman. You seem to have such a well-ordered life.'

Albert sighed. 'I thought I had, but my sister-in-law is presenting us with problems.'

'You mean because of Mr Alex and that young woman from the antiques shop?'

Albert was surprised and dismayed. He hadn't realized that the town knew of the disgrace.

'You know about the affair?'

'I'm afraid it's common knowledge, sir. That young Rosemary Wharton has an unsavoury reputation in the town. She's not really a local. She moved here from London so I'm told.'

She drained her glass and got to her feet.

'You've been most kind, sir. I promise I'll be back in the store by Friday.'

'If you have any problems with the school,' Albert said, 'give me a ring here at the store during the day.'

He didn't want her ringing him at home. Explanations to Jessie could be difficult.

Gripping the back of her chair she said again, 'You've been most kind and understanding, sir. I do appreciate it. I'd better get going now, that is, if you're sure I can leave the work.'

Albert got up too.

'Of course you can leave the work. Hang on a minute whilst I lock the safe and I'll drive you home.'

'Oh, there's no need for that, sir. I've taken up enough of your time already.'

He smiled at her. 'Then take up a little more of it. How long will it take me to drive you home? Wilbur Parade, isn't it?'

She was surprised that he remembered where she lived.

'Yes.'

She smiled and again he realized how pretty she was.

'It's what they call the evil belt, sir, between the sea and the canal.'

'Old wives' nonsense.'

'Oh, I don't know, sir. Lots of people believe it.'

Although it was a bleak February evening, Albert led his manageress out to the car with a strange feeling of excitement.

'Soon be spring, Laura,' he said as he handed her into the front passenger seat.

'Oh yes,' she said. 'It can't come too soon, can it? I hate February.'

From her tiny flat above the charity shop

27

opposite, Peggy Lambert, eighty-year-old widow who'd lived in Copmarsh all her life, watched them as they drove away from the store. Picking up one of her three cats and settling it on her lap she muttered to herself, 'Well, well, if it were anyone else but holy Joe Albie Freeman I'd have thought there was somethin' in it.' But he was probably running Laura Collins home because she was unwell. It was the sort of thing Albie Freeman *would* do. He'd always been a dull, holy Joe kind of chap, just living for his shop and the church choir. Give me a feller with fire in 'is belly, Peggy yearned, and she sighed for lost dreams.

CHAPTER THREE

Alex watched idly as she stepped into the brief frilly panties. His senses no longer leapt at the sight as they had done when he had first started his affair with Rosemary Wharton—the affair that had been so exciting at the start but which was beginning to pall.

She pouted prettily looking down at him as he sprawled on the bed.

'I can't see why you won't come to Tommy Preston's party.'

'I told you, Annabel doesn't care for local parties.'

'Come on your own then.'

'You know I can't do that.'

She sashayed over to him and sat down beside him on the bed, stroking his bare thigh.

'Why not? You came alone to the last one, the first time we met.'

'That was because Annabel went to a fashion show in Canterbury with Sally Soames and I was at a loose end.'

She snuggled up to him.

'And I just *love* your loose end.'

He shrugged away from her. He felt physically drained and faintly disgusted with himself. At first his affair with Rosemary had been exciting, something owing to him for allowing Annabel to bury him alive in the humdrum routine of life in the one-horse town of Copmarsh. Since his marriage he had found it difficult at times to get away for assignations with women in London and there had been resentment building up within him at the loss of his freedom. Annabel had tentatively suggested that they might start a family, but he had immediately rejected the idea. Surprisingly she had dropped the subject saying, 'Well, what you never have you never miss I suppose and I don't think I'm madly maternal anyway.'

He picked up his shirt from a chair beside Rosemary's bed and walked into the adjoining bathroom. As he made to close the door Rosemary stepped up to him clad only in bra and panties. Automatically his hand strayed to fondle one of the small pouting breasts. She seized his hand and kissed it.

'Don't go yet, lover.'

'I must. I have to get to the motorway and enter the town as if I've come down from London. I'm supposed to be working today.'

She backed away from him, frowning.

'I don't know why you bother with all this cloak-and-dagger stuff. Surely Annabel must suspect?'

He frowned. 'I don't want to hurt her any more than I have to. You must admit we've been a bit blatant lately. I can't go on inventing golf club committees and local property sales prospects indefinitely.'

'I don't see why not. Annabel can't prove you've been with *me*.'

He uttered a harsh laugh. 'You must be joking. You can't sneeze in this town without someone finding out, and that last time we had drinks in the Crown, two church cronies of my sainted brother-in-law were there. You can bet that news didn't take long to get to dear Albie.'

Rosemary gave a little snort. 'Who cares about Albie Freeman? He's about as sexless as . . . as . . .' She faltered, at a loss for words, then she said, 'the only thing that gives Albie Freeman an orgasm is when the church organist hits a wrong note on his precious organ.'

Alex felt revulsion at her vulgarity. He didn't like Albert Freeman, but he didn't care to listen to Rosemary's sneering remarks about

30

him. Also, he didn't care for lewd-talking women. All the females he had been involved with in the past had confined their lewdness to bed-play. Out of the bedroom they had been sophisticated, quiet-talking women, elegant and of unmistakably good breeding. Rosemary Wharton, he knew, was not one of them. She was what Annabel would call 'common'. All his innate snobbery revolted against Rosemary's coarse speech and flaunting sexuality. For a fleeting moment he thought of his wife. He had never known Annabel to lose her cool sophistication. He had never seen her composure ruffled. He guessed that was why Rosemary had, at first, seemed such a welcome romp, a relief from the flawless composure of his wife—so he excused himself.

He twisted away from the girl's clinging arm and closed the bathroom door on her. When he emerged a few minutes later she had put on pants and a smock top. She looked very young and vulnerable and, just for a second, he felt sorry for her. He had made up his mind to end the affair, but he didn't have the heart to tell her now. He would have to let her down gradually.

More subdued now she said, 'When will I see you again?'

'I'll give you a ring.'

'I could come up to Town in the daytime,' she offered eagerly. 'It's no problem. Molly Brown will cover for me in the shop.'

'Yes. Maybe that would be better than flaunting ourselves around locally. We've overdone it a bit lately. As I said before, I don't want Annabel to be hurt any more than necessary.'

Hurting Annabel Clifton was Rosemary's prime ambition. The sooner the snooty cow knew about the affair the better Rosemary would like it. Then maybe Alex would be spurred into action. She could visualize herself as mistress of his lovely house, entertaining exciting people from his London world to give the dull local residents of Copmarsh something to talk about besides flower shows, organ recitals and bring-and-buy sales. When Rosemary had left London in her teens with one divorce behind her and a modest income, she had chosen Copmarsh because, she calculated, it was better to be a big fish in a little pond than to set her sights too high. With her looks and personality she had thought it would be easy to capture the most exciting and well-heeled male, no matter if he belonged to someone else. Well, she had found the male, now it was up to her to carry out the rest of her life plan. Alex Clifton, she thought, is the most exciting man I've ever had. Not only was he extremely handsome, he had terrific charisma as well. She'd be crazy to let him get away.

'Ring me soon, lover.'

'Right.'

He picked up his briefcase and moved over

to the door. She pouted prettily.

'If I meet you in London, can we go to a hotel?'

'If I have time. I do have to work sometimes you know.'

'I thought you owned the firm.'

'I'm a partner, that's all, and I do have to account for my movements. If you come to Town I'll take you to lunch and put the bill on my expense account. No one will know that you aren't a prospective client.'

With a hint of desperation in her voice she said, 'I don't care if people *do* know about us.'

'Well, *I* do,' he answered her curtly. 'I'm respected in the firm and I rake in good business. I can't afford to let it be said that I'm allowing my philandering to interfere with the firm's profits.'

Again the pretty pout.

'I don't like that word—"philandering". I'd rather call it "love".'

Obviously eager to leave now, he turned on his way to the door and said with a short laugh, 'Love, my dear, is a many-sided object. Too much is covered by that waffle called love.'

When he had gone Rosemary drove down into the town to her shop. Molly Brown was just about to close when she arrived.

'Crumbs! I thought you'd have been too tired to come back in today.'

Rosemary grinned bleakly. 'I'm tough.'

Molly removed one of the more valuable

vases from the shop window and turned to her friend.

'Well, is he going to ask that stuck-up cow for a divorce?'

'You tell *me*.'

Cradling the vase to her chest Molly sank down on an antique chair, and eyed her friend critically.

'You've been crying. What's he done to you?'

'Tears of self-pity, that's all.' Rosemary sighed. 'I guess I'm too impatient.' She spread out her hands. 'These things take time. Men hate to be bulldozed into action.'

Molly uttered a curt laugh.

'He rushed into action all right when he wanted to get you into bed.'

'Not really. I helped him along. The first time I saw Alex Clifton I knew he was the one I'd been waiting for.'

'Yes, well . . .' Molly got up and placed the vase in a cabinet and locked the door. 'If you ask *me*, Alex Clifton isn't the type of guy to be content with one woman.'

'Well, I *didn't* ask you.'

Molly's voice was softer now.

'Listen, kiddo. Can you honestly see Alex Clifton giving up his ritzy lifestyle and his up-market wife for a casual affair?'

'It *wasn't* a casual affair.'

'*Wasn't?* Is it over then?'

'Of course not. Don't twist my words.'

Molly gazed at her friend with pity.

'Annabel Clifton is well liked and very much admired in this town and I can't see Dream Boy throwing his bonnet over the windmill for a casual fling.'

'And that's what you think it is? A casual fling?'

'I think that's how the town will see it and, if he's lucky, his precious Annabel.'

Rosemary moved and automatically straightened some antique dishes on a shelf.

'Well, it's up to him now. The town must know about us and I'm sure the saintly Albert and Jessie Freeman will be only too glad to boot him out of Annabel's life.'

'Yeh, maybe. Well, I'm off now if it's all right with you. I've got a class tonight.'

'OK. What is it? French or Italian?'

Molly rolled her eyes. 'Eye-talian. I plan to go to Rome in the summer and if I can't get laid by some gorgeous Eye-tye hunk this time, I'll go into a nunnery.'

Rosemary sighed as she locked the safe.

'Maybe I'd better go with you. Whipping Alex into action is going to be harder than I thought. By the way, any sales this afternoon?'

Molly shook her head.

'No. Just some old fart peering round asking if we had anything Japanese. Still, not to worry, this is a slow time of the year. When the spring comes trade is sure to look up but by that time, I guess, you'll be making wedding plans to rope in your precious Alex and then the shop can burn down for all you'll care.'

'I wish I could share your optimism.'

'Oh, come on now, Rosie. This isn't like you. You've never let a feller get you down before.'

'I've never met a feller like Alex Clifton before.' She sighed heavily. 'This time it's for real, Moll. I wish I could say it was the same for him.'

CHAPTER FOUR

Annabel looked round the bright spacious kitchen. She wondered how she would feel living in a small flat. Before her marriage she'd lived in her parents' large house with just one servant and, since her marriage, had lived here in her husband's family home with his two employees—cook, Gwen Lovell, and Gwen's husband Frank, gardener and general handyman. She knew she would have to tell them soon that she was leaving, but she owed it to Alex to tell him first. No doubt he would keep them on until he moved out or moved in his next woman. She didn't somehow think it would be Rosemary Wharton. Alex was a snob and the Wharton girl wasn't exactly top-drawer material. Well, it's no concern of mine, she told herself, all I can do is to retreat with dignity.

Gwen Lovell turned from the stove.

'Frank can't do much in the garden this

weather, madam, so he suggests he gets on with strengthening them fences termorrer, that is, if it's OK with Mr Alex, and get some creosote on 'em if the weather stays dry.'

'I'm sure that'll be fine,' said Annabel, smiling at the other woman. 'Why don't you and Frank take this evening off and go to visit your mother?' She gave a sniff of appreciation. 'It's casserole tonight, isn't it? I'm quite capable of dishing it up and loading the dishwasher afterwards. I'm sure you could do with a few hours off and I'm not certain what time my husband will be in tonight. It seems silly for you both to sit around here when I can easily manage on my own.'

'Well, if you're sure, madam,' said Gwen brightly. 'I know Mum would be thrilled if we popped in to see her and Frank can take Dad off for a game of darts in the Nelson's Arms. Dad's bin a bit down lately. That is, if you're sure you can manage, madam.'

Annabel regarded the other woman with genuine affection. She knew she would miss Gwen Lovell's comfortable presence.

'I'm more than sure I can manage, Gwen. You go off and get ready. Everything's under control here so that, when my husband comes in, all I have to do is to dish up.'

If only that were all, she thought dismally. The memory of her recent conversation with the Revd Knowles, Vicar of St Paul's, nagged at her.

'Would you like me to have a talk to Alex, my dear, point out to him, man-to-man, how foolish it is for him to be seen in local hostelries with Miss Wharton from the antiques shop? I'm sure it's all quite innocent, but people get the wrong ideas about these things and I think that if Alex was told that you could be hurt by local gossip, he'd be more careful in future.'

Annabel had told the Revd Knowles quite firmly that she didn't wish him to speak to Alex. 'It's my problem,' she'd told him firmly, 'and I'm quite capable of dealing with it thank you, Bernard, and his affair with the Wharton woman is certainly not "quite innocent" as you seem to think.'

The Revd Bernard Knowles had officiated at her marriage to Alex and although Annabel wasn't a regular church-goer like Jess, she did attend morning service occasionally and always went to church at Easter and Christmas, sometimes, but very rarely, accompanied by Alex. She knew that Jess and Albert occasionally entertained the Revd Bernard and his dull wife Mary, but Annabel and Alex had never been present on those occasions. Jess and Albert were obviously afraid that Alex would not have anything in common with Bernard and Mary Knowles and would deliberately be difficult.

Well, Jess had warned her not to marry Alex Clifton. I realize now, Annabel thought, how very much like Mum Jess is. The voice of doom, sour wisdom, but always so very right. I was a fool to think I could rebel against it.

She left the kitchen and went back upstairs. Her precious jewellery she had put into the bank. Now there was just the costume jewellery to deal with. Most of this was also quite valuable, but not so valuable as to be at great risk. Once she was established in her new home she would see that there was security for her valuables because she did not believe in owning beautiful jewellery and being afraid to wear it. Besides, she would need it in her new life. She did not intend to sit at home, the discarded wife. She was determined to make a social life of her own. No one in Copmarsh would be able to pity her as a sorrowing victim. Even so, after she had placed her jewellery into cases, storing the cases into a leather vanity bag, a sudden huge depression swamped her. No matter how brave a face she put on, she would still be a failed wife—a reject. She looked at her diamond wristwatch, a present from Alex at their engagement. Soon he would be home and then their marriage would be over. Thank goodness there were no children involved.

She needed a drink. As she went downstairs she heard the Lovells' car going down the drive so they would be out for the rest of the evening. They were lucky. They had each other. She mixed herself a double martini, laced with ice and olives, and sat down to wait. He came in just after six, handsome, assured, with the slight swagger that made him so attractive. She was, by then, on her second large martini. He tossed his briefcase on to the settee and sank down on a chair. He threw her the usual smile accompanied by a kiss-twist of his mouth which usually made her heart leap with love and excitement. This evening, however, she braced herself against the usual reaction.

'Had a good day, sweetheart?'

Annabel smiled sweetly at him.

'Yes thanks. A very good day. I've seen a flat I intend to move into.'

'You've what?'

She got up and moved to the sideboard. Her body was trembling, but she fought to stay calm. She turned with her fingers round the top of the gin bottle.

'Your usual?'

'I'll do it myself, thanks.' He got up and moved over to her. 'Did I hear you wanted us to move?'

He was close to her now—too close for comfort. She moved out of his reach and went back to the settee.

'No. You didn't hear me say I wanted *us* to move; you heard me say *I* was going to move.'

'Are you mad?'

'No. Just stupid, but that's going to change now. I'm no longer the silly trusting laughing-stock of Copmarsh.'

He slopped a generous measure of gin into his glass and glared at her.

'What on earth are you talking about? Are you drunk, Annabel?'

She took a sip of her drink before she answered him.

'Rosemary Wharton.'

'What about Rosemary Wharton?'

With a calm she was far from feeling she replied, 'Do you need to ask me that?'

He gave a harsh laugh.

'Oh, I see. The old grapevine's been humming again, has it? I bought the woman a drink or two. She's thinking about selling her shop and buying a property locally. The one she's in now is only rented.'

He looked away from the miserable derision in his wife's eyes as he topped up his drink.

'Does she need to buy a property? Won't she be moving in here when I go?'

Alex took a deep swallow of his drink, then went back to sit down facing her.

'Now, look here, Annabel, what's all this about? I sense dear Jessie's hand in this nonsense. You know I have to entertain prospective clients. You've never objected before.'

'You've never paraded your women locally before.'

'My women? What the hell do you mean by my women?'

She stared at him determined not to weaken.

'Oh, I know there have been plenty and I thought it was a phase which would pass, but

41

when it comes to humiliating me in my home town, I find I can't take it any more.'

He put his glass down on a small table, got up and went over to sit beside her on the settee. He tried to put an arm round her, but she shrugged away from his embrace.

'You can't sweet-talk me out of it this time, Alex. Our marriage is over and it's up to us to end it with dignity. I have no intention of moving away from Copmarsh unless I have to, but I'd like a divorce as quickly as possible so that I can get on with my life. I've no intention of going into retirement as the discarded wronged wife. I intend to live a little now, and to hell with what people say. The town is big enough for both of us and I don't intend to give the gossips the satisfaction of watching us fighting. When our social paths cross in future it will be up to us to take it in our stride and greet each other with civility like old friends.'

He stared at her in stark horror.

'Old friends? We're lovers, damn it!'

She threw him a miserable smile.

'*Were* lovers.'

She took a deep swallow of her drink and her smile was bright now as she faced him.

'It's funny really. I've never taken much notice of Jessie's advice, but now I realize that she was right when she said our marriage wouldn't work.'

Alex ran a hand distractedly through his thick hair.

'What does that silly bitch know about life?'

'Enough to get herself a happy marriage to a good, faithful man.'

Alex gave a harsh laugh. 'Would *you* like to be married to dear Albert?'

Annabel smiled. 'No. I intend to find myself trendier talent than Albert Freeman.'

'Trendier talent? You're talking like a bloody teenager.'

If she hadn't been so desperately unhappy Annabel would have enjoyed her husband's shock. His cosy world had turned turtle on him and he didn't know how to handle it. Alex Clifton, the darling of the women, the envy of the men, was at a loss.

'I'm seeing Mr Botham tomorrow morning,' she said, 'to institute divorce proceedings.'

Alex tried again to put his arm around her, but she got up from the settee, went over to the sideboard and poured another drink.

'You're drunk,' he said. 'You never drink this much. You don't know what you're saying.'

'Oh yes I do,' she said calmly. 'I know very well what I'm saying. Our phoney marriage is over, my dear Alex, and the sooner you do something about it, the better. I suggest you use one of your slick London lawyers to help you. I don't intend to make any financial claims on you.'

Alex put his hands over his head. His voice was muffled.

'I can't believe I'm hearing this. I thought we

had a wonderful marriage. I love you, Annabel; I don't want to live with any other woman.'

'I believe you, Alex. I think it would suit you very well to live with me just so long as you can go out to play when you feel like it.'

He raised his head and regarded her with haggard eyes.

'*Please*, darling, give me another chance. I promise not to see Rosemary Wharton again, even though it was all in the course of business. From now on . . .'

'It's no good, Alex.' Her voice was perfectly controlled now. She found she was no longer trembling. She had come this far. She had to see it through to the end. 'It's too late. The damage is done and my mind is made up. I can't go around Copmarsh knowing that people are seeing me as a blind fool.'

She put down her drink and moved to the door.

'Your dinner is in the oven. All you have to do is to dish it up. Then, when you've finished, load the dish-washer.'

He stared at her in miserable amazement.

'Where are you going?'

'I'm dining out. I've given the Lovells the evening off. I expect to be home about eleven. Tomorrow, after you've gone to work, I'll tell them we've split up and that I'm leaving straight away. To avoid any awkwardness I'm moving into a hotel until my flat is ready.'

He shook his head despairingly.

'I can't believe I'm hearing all this.'

She smiled thinly. 'No. It is a bit final, isn't it?'

'Annabel, *please*. Sit down and let's talk this thing through.'

'No, Alex. My mind is made up. If you need to get a message to me, ring Pepper Finlay at the Crown.'

'Pepper Finlay? What's she got to do with us? She's a tart.'

Annabel's eyebrows shot up.

'Compared with Rosemary Wharton, Pepper is a lady. Anyway, Pep and I are old school chums and she will see that I get any messages you want to send me.'

He walked over to her, but she whirled away from his attempted embrace.

'Annabel, *please*. Don't go. Sit down and let's talk this through like civilized adults.'

'It's too late for that, Alex. I've been a civilized adult too long.'

He groaned. 'I just can't believe this is happening. I thought we were so right for each other.'

'So did I. Once.'

'You say Pepper Finlay will take your messages. Will you be staying at the Crown then?'

'Yes. I've packed all my clothes and jewellery and I'll get it all round to the Crown tomorrow after I've told Frank and Gwen Lovell that we are parting. I presume they'll stay on with you

45

unless and until you make other arrangements.'

'You've got it all worked out, haven't you?' he said bitterly. 'I hope you realize that throwing yourself on Pepper Finlay's mercy won't do your reputation any good in the town.'

'Pepper runs a highly prestigious hotel,' said Annabel. 'The Crown is the best hostelry in the district. I'm quite sure that staying there for a spell won't harm my reputation in the town. In fact, I'll be dining there this evening with Pepper.'

'So dear Pepper will be washing our dirty linen all over town.'

Annabel looked at him steadily.

'Our linen was made dirty by you in the first place, Alex. I can't see that Pepper will make it any worse. Anyhow, I'm sure she'll be the soul of discretion.'

Alex uttered a bitter laugh. 'Just like she has been with her own affairs.'

'Pepper's affairs haven't broken up any marriages that weren't on the rocks already.'

'You can't say our marriage is on the rocks because of one small stupid indiscretion.'

Annabel laughed curtly. 'I doubt if Rosemary Wharton regards it as a small stupid indiscretion.'

'Rosemary Wharton doesn't count. It's you I want, Annabel. I love you.'

She threw him a tiny smile as she opened the door.

'Too late, Alex, I'm afraid. Enjoy your

dinner. I'll see you around.'

She picked up her overnight case in the hall and went out to the garage to get her car. It was a cold, starry night and she shivered. February was a horrid month, but soon it would be spring. Spring—the time for hope and love. Now she had no love, but, thank God, she could still hope. Even so tears stained her cheeks as she let herself into the garage and there was a cold chill in her heart.

CHAPTER FIVE

Jessie waited until the maid had left the room before she spoke. Albert took a careful sip of his red wine before tackling the prawn cocktail which had been put before him. The sherries he'd enjoyed with Laura Collins had made him just the slightest bit tipsy. Jessie's voice cut sharply into his pleasant euphoria.

'Annabel's moving into that flat in Romney Place at the end of this week. It seems she can't get away from Alex quickly enough.'

'Well,' said Albert, 'if she's made up her mind to leave him there's no point in delaying it I suppose.'

'There has to be some other way. I did think that perhaps you might talk to him.'

Alfred stopped prodding his prawn cocktail with a spoon and looked up sharply.

'*Me* talk to Alex? I've nothing in common with the fellow. I've never liked him. I didn't approve of Annabel marrying him in the first place.'

'She's going to divorce him.'

Albert was surprised. Separation was one thing, but divorce, in his opinion, was a bit drastic.

'Why would she want to divorce him? It's probably only a temporary lapse. She would do better to ignore it like a lady.'

Jessie pushed her plate away from her. She regarded her husband with worried eyes.

'She's changed, Albert. She's gone all common and flippant, just like that awful Pepper Finlay from the Crown. She's staying at the Crown until she moves into her flat and Pepper Finlay's helping her buy furniture. She's talking like a stranger, Albert—said she's going to have some fun for a change. I shudder to think what she meant. I invited her to come to us for a spell, but she said she'd prefer to take a room in Pepper Finlay's hotel. I hate to think of that woman's influence over Annabel in Annabel's frame of mind.'

Sensing that Albert was not giving her his full attention, Jessie went on, 'Annabel should give some thought to *your* position in the town, Albert. A prominent businessman like you commands respect, but with a sister-in-law peddling her matrimonial troubles with a woman like Pepper Finlay and then seeking a divorce, well, that's not going to do you much good in the town, is it?'

'Oh, I don't think it'll harm *me*, Jess,' said Albert, thinking of the way Laura Collins had looked this evening when she had thanked him for driving her home. 'Divorce is no big deal these days.'

'No big deal?' Jessie's voice was sharp. '*I* think it's a *very* big deal. There's never been a divorce in my family, or in yours.'

Albert spooned up some of the prawn cocktail. He needed to get some food in his belly so that he could savour the red wine he always enjoyed with his dinner. This evening's pre-dinner sherries had upset his metabolism. He looked across at his wife's plain, worried face and again the serene smile of Laura Collins bugged him.

'My dear Jessie,' he said, 'what Alex and Annabel do can't be blamed on us. Now, try to stop worrying about your sister and let's get on with our dinner. By the way, those new cushions you ordered came in today. I'll have Miss Collins' assistant unpack them for you tomorrow.' It gave him a faint thrill to speak her name.

But Jessie's mind was not on cushions or Miss Collins. Her husband's attitude disconcerted her. Albert was usually very sympathetic to her criticisms of Alex and Annabel, but tonight he seemed indifferent almost. She wondered if something had gone

49

wrong at the store.

'Was everything all right today at the store, Albert?'

He looked up, a strange feeling of guilt riding him.

'Of course it was. Why shouldn't it be?'

'No reason. It's just that you seem a bit . . .'

'A bit what?'

'I don't know exactly. You didn't seem all that bothered when I told you that Annabel's seeking a divorce.'

He smiled at his wife, thinking that Jess should do a bit more to make herself attractive. Her hair-do was awful and a little colouring in her hair wouldn't come amiss to hide the fast-encroaching grey.

'As I said before, dear, Annabel's divorce can't be blamed on us. We all have a cross to bear of some sort in our lives.' He thought of poor Laura Collins and *her* cross. More gently now he added, 'I'm sure people won't blame us for Annabel's behaviour and the divorce will probably go through quietly if it's uncontested.'

'And you're just going to sit back and do nothing?'

He made a face. 'There's too much dressing on this prawn cocktail. Maisie knows I don't like too much of it.' Jessie tried to hide her impatience.

'All right, I'll speak to her about it later. I asked, Albert, if you're just going to sit back and do nothing.'

He smiled at her, realizing that he was being a bit grouchy this evening.

'About what dear?'

'Oh, Albert, for Heaven's sake! What's the matter with you tonight? We were talking about Alex and Annabel.'

'No dear. *You* were talking about Alex and Annabel.'

Jessie was really riled now. Albert was behaving so much out of character tonight. If she hadn't known him better, she'd have thought he'd been drinking.

'So you don't care if Annabel brings the family into disgrace?'

Albert gave her a smile which was intended to be comforting, but instead came over as patronizing.

'There's hardly any family to be considered, Jess. There's only you and me. There are no children involved, which *is* a blessing.'

'So, do I take it that you refuse to have a talk with Alex?'

Albert was, by now, persevering with his prawn cocktail.

'Eat your dinner, Jess. It doesn't do your digestion any good to get steamed up about something that isn't really our business.'

'Not our business? We're the only family Annabel has, for Heaven's sake.'

'Well, she didn't ask our permission to marry Alex Clifton; she certainly won't need our permission to end the marriage. Stop worrying,

Jess, and leave Annabel to sort out her own problems. I'm sure she's more than capable.'

'Egged on by that awful Pepper Finlay.'

'Oh, the woman's not so bad. Does a lot for charity I understand.'

Jessie pushed her prawn cocktail away and stared at her husband. She had a strange feeling of disquiet. She had always been able to rely on Albert agreeing with her on all important issues and it seemed unbelievable that he was letting her down now.

'Annabel is my baby sister, Albert. I can't stand by and watch her being thrown to the wolves.'

Albert gave a little snigger.

'Isn't that being rather dramatic, Jess? Eat your dinner, dear. Maisie will be in with the main course any minute now.'

But Jessie was near to tears. Her world was crumbling around her. First, her sister, now her husband. If only Mum were still alive. She'd sort them out. When the maid came in with the main course Jessie handed back her prawn cocktail untouched.

'Something wrong, madam?' the girl asked fearfully.

'Yes. Too much dressing.'

The girl was troubled. 'I'm sorry, madam. I did it the way I always do it. You've never complained before.'

'Oh, forget it, Maisie,' Jessie snapped. 'We'll talk about it later. Just leave the vegetables on

52

the table. We'll help ourselves.'

'Very good, madam.'

The girl was clearly huffed. Albert threw her an apologetic half smile as she left the room. Jessie saw it. It was another link in his betrayal.

*   *   *

Pepper Finlay and Annabel Clifton were finishing dinner in a corner of the Crown Hotel's elegant dining-room and were now on their liqueurs. Both women looked sensational dressed in black with glamorous hair-dos and sparkling gems in their ears.

Several patrons had stopped at their table during the evening to exchange pleasantries, openly curious at seeing the two women dining together with no men-folk.

'Well Pep,' said Annabel. 'You must admit the Cliftons have put the Crown on the map for you, what with Alex blatantly drinking in here with Rosemary Wharton and now me dining here without him. We're certainly giving the locals food for thought.'

Pepper grinned. 'Just like the old days at school, eh? Remember old Ma Barnes tapping the front desk with that pointer of hers."Annabel Stanton and Pepper Dale, may we all share the joke? Maybe you'd like to take the class whilst I have a rest. You seem to have plenty to say. Let us all hear it and maybe we'll learn something".'

Annabel giggled. 'Yes. Right old trout, wasn't she? She was always telling me what a paragon of virtue Jessie was and how she couldn't understand a studious, obedient girl like Jessie Stanton having me for a sister. Jess always stood up for me, though. I'll give her that. She still does today, although she hates the idea of me divorcing Alex.' She sighed. 'Poor Alex. I wonder how he is? He was quite unprepared for this. I'm fairly sure he doesn't really want Rosemary Wharton on a long-term basis.'

'I'm damn sure he doesn't,' said Pepper. 'What an idiot he was to bring her in here for drinks. He must have known it would be all over town in a flash.'

Annabel's eyes darkened. 'Yes. That's what bugs *me*—his arrogance. He'd got to the stage where he thought he could take chances. He didn't think I'd ever rear up and take action against his philandering.'

She smiled at her friend.

'I don't know how I'd ever have got through this without you, Pep. I guess I'd just have sat back listening to Jess and Albert telling me it would be more ladylike to ignore my husband's whoring and preserve my dignity in the town.'

'As so many misguided women have done before you,' said Pepper gently. 'But those days of women being second-class citizens are over, thank God. We have as much right as the men to lead fulfilled lives.'

Annabel raised her brandy goblet to her friend.

'Here's to fulfilment then and lots of it.'

Pepper laughed as she lifted her own goblet.

'To us and it's only just beginning, Annie, you'll see.'

'To us.' Annabel sipped her brandy with a smile, but her heart was as bleak as the February weather outside.

CHAPTER SIX

David Seymour was forty years old and, since his divorce twelve years before, had been managing the Crown for Pepper Finlay. Pepper's divorced husband, now living in the USA with his new wife, had been a school-friend of David's. David and Pepper had met quite by chance at a party given by a mutual friend when both were at a loose end after finalizing their respective divorces. Pepper had discussed with David her decision to keep on the upmarket Crown Hotel in the marshland surrounding the small town of Copmarsh which she had run very profitably with her ex-husband since their marriage. 'But without a man,' she told David, 'I feel I might not be able to cope, staff and tradesmen might try to sell me short. What I need is a man, but I never want another marriage or serious relationship again. I find I like my life to myself now that all the heartache guff is over.'

It had seemed the obvious thing for David Seymour to offer himself as manager of Pepper's hotel, especially as he had been brought up in a hotel owned by his parents on the south coast. He was fortunate enough to have an adequate income from his deceased parents so that he was content to take a modest salary at first. Later, as the prosperity of the hotel increased, Pepper insisted on his having a share of the profits. It was an admirable arrangement. They respected each other's private lives and each other's expertise— David's in hotel management, Pepper's in the glamorous side of the business. Between them they had built up a hotel which was not only very prestigious in the town of Copmarsh and surrounding district, but also much further afield. People came from London and the hotel also attracted visitors from abroad. French and Americans often stayed there enjoying its luxurious accommodation and the excellent menus, whilst also thrilling to the legends of the awesome marshland with its stories of past smugglers and avenging revenue men.

As for David and Pepper, their relationship was rather like that of brother and sister. They were there for each other when problems arose and there was a genuine nonsexual charisma between them. Pepper knew that David had brief affairs with various women, but these short flings were never allowed to interfere with his duties as hotel manager, and he never blatantly displayed his women before Pepper. As for Pepper, since her divorce she'd indulged in a few very short sexual adventures, but these were always conducted well out of range of the hotel.

During Annabel Clifton's short stay at the Crown after leaving her husband, she got to know David Seymour quite well. Sometimes he would join Annabel and Pepper for meals and they would discuss the small town's history. David had done a lot of research into old records and they laughed together over stories of past vicars and squires who had been involved in smuggling operations.

The night before Annabel was to leave the hotel to move into her flat, the three of them were having what Pepper called 'the last supper' together.

'I wonder how your dear brother-in-law would have reacted,' said Pepper to Annabel, 'if his respected vicar had been on the receiving end of the smuggling.'

'Turned a blind eye and said twice as many prayers,' suggested David with a grin.

Pepper smiled. 'Poor Albert, I don't know who I pity most, Albert or Jess.'

'They neither of them need your pity,' said Annabel, 'they lead very satisfying, respectable lives.'

'Oh, come off it,' Pepper scoffed. 'I bet dear

Albert has the odd urge when he's sorting out the ladies' underwear in that mausoleum of his, surrounded by his prissy assistants. That shop of his should go into Madam Tussaud's when Albert dies. It's like something out of *Oliver Twist*.'

'Oh, it's not too bad these days,' laughed Annabel. 'Albert's gradually coming into present-day trading—T-shirts, jeans and duvet covers. They almost gave him a coronary, but I think he's adjusted now.'

Pepper laughed. 'But dear old Jess still sticks to the twin sets and pearls, doesn't she?'

Annabel giggled with her friend.

'Yes. Jess will never change. She's so like our mother, always has a quotation for every situation. "Two wrongs don't make a right, Annabel", "Look before you leap, Annabel". Oh God, she remembers them all. Sometimes I want to yell at her, but then I know she's really very concerned about me and I'm ashamed of myself.'

'Well, that's all in the past,' said Pepper briskly. 'Tomorrow you start a new life in your new home and to hell with Jess and her isms.'

Annabel's eyes clouded for a second, then she smiled.

'Yes. A new start and as soon as all the furniture's in and I'm settled, I intend to have a house-warming party.'

'Splendid,' said Pepper, 'and shall you invite dear Albert and Jess?'

58

'Of course, but I don't think they'll come.'

'You never know,' said Pepper, 'they might surprise you.' She paused, then she said quietly, 'And Alex?'

David flashed a quick frown at her and she was afraid she'd overstepped the mark, but Annabel just grinned and said, 'Why not? And Rosemary Wharton too, for good measure. That should shock the pants right off Copmarsh. Imagine the gossip in the coffee shops.' She threw back her head and her smile was brilliant. 'What a good idea. I can't wait.' She lifted her glass. 'Let's drink then, to the first civilized divorce in Copmarsh.'

David and Pepper exchanged quick glances as they raised their glasses in the toast.

'To Annabel Clifton,' Pepper said, 'and her new lifestyle.'

David drank slowly, looking all the time at Annabel, realizing at last just how very beautiful she was. He had never really taken a lot of notice of her before. He had seen her as the smiling, placid wife of the dashing Alex Clifton, always in the shadow of her dynamic husband. Sometimes, very rarely, Alex and Annabel had dined at the Crown, but always then she had been in the background, the ideal supportive consort for her man. Tonight David was seeing her in her own right, a seductive and very vulnerable woman. As he drank the toast now he said, 'To Annabel and her new life. May it be a happy one.'

59

She smiled across at him.

'Well, at least it should be an interesting one, David. You see, I'll be living in what they call the evil belt now, between the sea and the canal. It's reputed to be spooked.'

Pepper laughed. 'Surely you don't believe that stupid old story, Annie?'

'Oh yes I do,' said Annabel seriously, 'but it doesn't put me off. It might be fun for a change.'

'So the superstition doesn't scare you?'

Annabel giggled.

'No. I've got my grandmother's ivory crucifix to hold in my hand if the going gets too tough.'

They were all three silent for a moment, then Pepper signalled to a hovering waiter.

'Same again all round, please Ray.'

When the fresh drinks came they raised their glasses.

'To us,' David said. 'And may we all flourish like the good old bay tree.'

Pepper looked surprised.

'Isn't that something from the Bible, David?'

'Yes. It's from Psalms, Pep, all about the ungodly flourishing like the green bay tree.'

Pepper looked serious for a second, then she laughed. 'You've got hidden depths, David my dear. I didn't know you were religious.'

'Oh, I went to Sunday school,' said David flippantly.

Annabel was silent. Tomorrow she would start a new life alone and she was afraid.

Albert Freeman sat in his glass-enclosed office idly watching the scene below. Already the weather showed occasional glimpses of spring and customers were beginning to take interest in the new display of T-shirts and jeans. He still couldn't help feeling regret for the demise of the lacy blouse and pretty skirts which, it appeared, were no longer in vogue. He felt a little disorientated today. It seemed strange not to see Laura Collins in her customary seat in the store, but her telephone call a while ago had pleased him. She told him that she'd had a long talk with her son and her son's headmaster and no disciplinary action would be taken against the boy for this his first offence.

'I'm coming back tomorrow,' she'd said. 'There's no point in my staying on here.'

'Take your time, Laura,' he'd told her. 'Stay longer if you need to, not that we shan't be glad to see you back here.' He had been going to say '*I* shan't be glad . . .' but substituted the 'we', afraid of embarrassing her.

Tomorrow his sister-in-law would be moving into her flat in Romney Place so he guessed that tonight at dinner Jessie would be making it the sole topic of her conversation. He knew that Jessie had been hurt a lot by Annabel's decision to move temporarily into the Crown

Hotel instead of staying with them, but he was relieved that Annabel had saved him the embarrassment of harbouring her after her surprising walk-out on her husband. Granted he had no time for Alex Clifton and if Annabel could cut adrift from him without too much scandal, Albert thought it would be a good thing.

'For her to go and stay with that Pepper Finlay,' Jessie had stormed, 'is the last straw. What will people think?'

'Does it matter?' Albert had said. He himself had watched Pepper Finlay in the past with grudging admiration, almost like a small boy looking at pictures of nudes. Of course, he didn't approve of her lifestyle, but one had to admit that she was a damned attractive woman, and he was glad Annabel had elected to go to her after her walk-out on Alex. It had saved Jessie and himself from involvement. Pity Jess couldn't see it that way.

He sighed as he looked at the gold pocket-watch he had inherited from his father. Soon be time to go home and listen to Jess bemoaning the fact that her sister was moving into the so-called evil belt between the sea and the canal. He gathered his papers and put them away. Strange how empty the store seemed without Laura moving about her customary duties. Ah well, he said silently, to quote the writer of the famous *Gone with the Wind*, 'Tomorrow is another day'.

CHAPTER SEVEN

The Copmarsh grapevine operated swiftly. Annabel's farewell to her husband's servants, Frank and Gwen Lovell, had immediate results. Both Frank and Gwen were genuinely upset at the news of Annabel's departure. 'No one is really to blame,' she told them. 'Mr Alex and I have realized that we were not suited to run in harness and we think it better that we should part. I think I shall continue to live in Copmarsh and, as far as I know, my husband will continue to live here, so I don't think it will affect you too much.'

The couple had liked working for Annabel She had been a kind, undemanding mistress and they were apprehensive about the future, especially if Alex Clifton moved in the tarty Rosemary Wharton. They had heard the rumours flying around about his affair with the proprietress of the antiques shop and thought him a fool to put a good marriage on the rocks for a woman of loose morals. They had not been told to keep the matter secret and, naturally, talked to local traders about the split-up of their employers. It was inevitable that Rosemary Wharton should hear of it. The news had been imparted to Molly Brown by the window-cleaner.

At first Rosemary was delighted, but then dismayed and shocked because the news hadn't reached her via Alex. She knew it was no use telephoning him at home during the daytime, so she looked up his London phone number.

Molly Brown was openly dubious.

'Won't he mind you ringing him at work?'

'I shall say I'm ringing about a property in Copmarsh if they ask me.'

'He might not like it.'

'Too bad. He likes what I give him. Anyway, I guess he'd have told me himself if he'd had time.'

She tried to push away the feeling of shock Molly's news had given her. *Why* hadn't Alex told her immediately? She should have been the first to know as she was obviously the cause of the break-up.

'If I was you I'd give him a bit of breathing space,' suggested Molly. 'He probably doesn't realize yet just what's hit him.'

But Rosemary was past accepting advice. She *had* to talk to Alex, and now. She dialled the number and asked to speak to him.

A subdued, cultured voice at the other end told her, 'I'm afraid Mr Clifton is out. Could anyone else help you?'

'No. I have to speak to Mr Clifton. When will he be in?'

There was a slight pause, then the careful voice replied, 'I'm not quite sure. Mr Clifton is lunching with a client. If you'll give me your number, I'll ask him to call when he returns.'

Rosemary's heart sank. Was it a woman Alex was lunching with? She gave her number and the voice at the other end asked, 'Could you give me some idea of why you wish to speak to Mr Clifton?'

Nosy cow! Rosemary had a job to stop herself from saying the words aloud. Instead she replied curtly, 'It's about a property in Copmarsh. I'd be obliged if you'd get him to ring me immediately he gets in. It's urgent.' And she put the phone down.

'Trouble?' queried Molly innocently.

'One of those bloody Sloane Rangers by the sound of it,' snapped Rosemary. 'The kind that works for fun.'

'Yeh. I guess he must meet a lot of 'em in his line of business,' said Molly dreamily, 'him being so rich and good-looking and all.'

The day dragged for Rosemary. The phone rang once and she dashed to answer it, only to receive an enquiry about some porcelain from a man in Canterbury. She handed over the phone to Molly Brown with instructions to 'Keep it brief. I want the line kept free'. The day dragged by, but there was no call from Alex. When she got home she waited until seven o'clock, then she rang his house. Gwen Lovell answered, telling her that Mr Alex was staying in London this evening and wasn't sure when he'd be returning to Copmarsh.

'May I give him a message for when he rings

again?' the woman asked. 'I'm expecting him to call me tomorrow morning.'

'Yes,' said Rosemary, 'ask him to ring 259374; it's a local number and be sure to tell him it's extremely urgent please.'

As she replaced the phone she didn't know whether to scream with frustration or cry. She was sure the Lovell woman knew about Alex Clifton's affair with her and was probably sniggering right now. She mooched into her sitting-room and poured herself a large Scotch. She carried it to a small table beside the sofa and sank down, resigned to an evening of quiet misery. Why hadn't Alex got in touch with her and told her that Annabel had left him? Was he spending the evening with the woman he'd lunched with? If it *had* been a woman, but Rosemary was fairly sure it was. This should be the happiest day of my life, she thought, why then do I feel so scared?

Alex Clifton was not her first lover since her divorce, but she realized now that he was the only man she'd ever loved.

She was quite drunk by the time she went to bed, although her mind was crystal clear. She was afraid to take sleeping pills after all the strong drink she'd consumed, so she spent the entire night cat-napping with ghastly dreams. In the morning she arrived at the shop by 8.30 determined to be there to receive the call from Alex when it came, *if* it came.

Molly Brown pretended to stagger back in

shock when she found the shop door unlocked and Rosemary standing just inside.

'Blimey! Where's the fire? You look awful. A night of passion or too much grog?'

She received no answering smile from her employer.

'Neither,' Rosemary snapped. 'I came in early because Alex is ringing me this morning.'

'Oh. You managed to contact him then?'

Rosemary didn't answer. She turned and went back to slump down in a chair behind the desk. A cup of coffee stood on the desk top beside her.

'Want a cuppa?'

'Yes,' replied Molly. 'Don't get up; I'll do it myself.'

When she came back into the shop with her coffee she sat down beside her employer.

'You look awful, Rosie. What's the matter?'

Tears started in the other woman's eyes.

'I'm so scared, Moll.'

'Scared? What of? You ought to be laughing. You got rid of the opposition without even a fight.'

'But why hasn't he told me?'

'Maybe he wants to surprise you.'

Rosemary snorted. 'I doubt it. He's not the type to spring itty-bitty surprises.'

Molly sipped her coffee and eyed Rosemary warily.

'Will you move in with him, or will he move in with you now that she's gone?'

Rosemary shook her head.

'You tell *me*. He hasn't even told me she's gone. I had to hear it from your friend, the window-cleaner, didn't I? Alex hasn't told me.'

'Can't you just ring and ask him?'

'I've phoned his office and the house. He didn't come home last night. The housekeeper said he was staying in London. He's never done that before, at least not since I've known him.'

Rosemary stared at her assistant with bleak eyes. 'Why hasn't he called me, Moll? You'd think I'd be the first to know she'd left, specially seeing as how I'm the cause of the break-up. Oh God, why doesn't he ring me?'

Molly glanced at her watch.

'Well, give him a chance. It's early yet. If he's staying in Town he's probably not up yet. Has he got a flat in Town?'

Rosemary shook her head. 'I don't think so. He's got a club.'

'Well, that's where he'll be then.'

'I wish I could believe that.'

'Well, where else would he be? He wouldn't sleep in the office. He hasn't got a bird in Town has he?'

'I don't know,' replied Rosemary miserably. 'That office bitch said he was lunching with someone yesterday.'

'A woman?'

'She didn't say, but I bet it was.'

'Now, don't go jumping to conclusions, Rosie, it won't do you any good.' She gave a

68

little grin. 'Just be patient. He's probably planning to take you out somewhere posh to tell you the good news.'

Rosemary smiled feebly. 'I wish I could believe that.'

'Believe it and, buck up, Rosie. You don't want to let him know you've been crying. Men get bored with tears. Besides, you've got rid of the opposition, now the road's all clear for you.' Suddenly sobered, she added, 'Will you get rid of the shop when you get together with *him*?'

Rosemary looked surprised. 'I hadn't really thought about it. Yes, I guess I will. I shan't need to work when I'm married to *him*.'

She dashed the tears from her eyes and attempted a smile.

'Just think, a lady of leisure, married to the dishiest male in Kent.'

Molly looked worried. 'I was wond'ring, would you consider keeping on the shop and making me the manageress? You wouldn't need to come in very often and you know I'd take good care of the business. I wouldn't slack or cheat you.' Her voice faltered a little. 'I don't know where else I'd go for a job. People round here are so narrow-minded and clannish and if they're buddies of Annabel Clifton they might not take too kindly to me, you see . . .'

Rosemary interrupted her, trying to muster a smile, 'Oh, Moll. What a selfish cow I am. I was so wrapped up in my own affairs that I never gave a thought to you. Yes, of course I'll keep on the shop.' Her smile brightened. 'Maybe, if you start saving now, you could afford to buy the business off me. After all, I won't exactly be hard up. I might be able to let you have it at a knockdown figure, provided you kept all the best snips for *me*.'

Soon they were both laughing, but Rosemary's heart was still heavy with foreboding and the day dragged through with still no phone call from Alex.

*   *   *

Albert Freeman looked up as a shadow fell across the glass window of his tiny office. He slid off his stool and eagerly opened the door to Laura Collins. It was 4 p.m. and he had given up all hope of seeing her today. He was taken aback by her appearance. It was a cold February day, but bright with sunshine and her thick, short-jacketed, wine-coloured suit looked just right for a winter's day verging on spring. She looked, he thought, extremely elegant in quiet good taste.

'Why, Laura, come in. How good to see you. Would you like some tea? I can get one of the girls to make it.'

'No thanks Mr Freeman. I've just got off the bus from the station. I *was* going straight home, then I thought I ought to pop in to tell you that I'm back and will be in to work tomorrow.'

'I'm very glad you did, Laura. Are you sure

you feel like coming in tomorrow?'

'Oh yes, Mr Freeman. I've no reason to stay at home. Besides, this place is my life.'

There was a strange feeling taking hold of Albert. It was like a glow, he thought. 'This place is my life, she'd said. Well, it was *his* life, too, the most important thing in his life, and this woman appreciated it, unlike his wife and his younger employees who just regarded it as a job.

'Well, we've missed you,' he said, 'but I'm so glad you were able to settle things so quickly. Are you really happy about the boy now?'

Her eyes clouded slightly. 'Not happy exactly, but he's promised it won't happen again. I'm afraid I threatened to get in touch with his father and that seemed to distress him so I said I wouldn't, not unless it happens again that is.'

Albert felt a stab of dismay. 'You surely wouldn't get in touch with that man again after all this time, would you Laura?'

She gave a little shrug. 'I'd much rather not. Besides, it might cause unhappiness to his present family and I wouldn't want that to happen.'

No, she wouldn't, he decided, she was far too nice a woman to want to hurt anyone.

'Well, I mustn't hold up your work, Mr Freeman. I only just popped in to . . .'

He cut her short, anxious to detain her as long as possible. 'You are not holding up my

71

work, Laura. In fact, I had almost decided to stay late this evening, some checking I need to do.'

She looked surprised and a little worried. 'Something wrong, Mr Freeman?'

He gave her a reassuring smile. 'No. Just a silly notion of mine. I thought I'd get out some old records of the years before we started selling these'—he looked slightly disdainful—'these jeans and T-shirt things, etcetera, just to see if they are more profitable than the dignified wares for which the store has long been famous. I realize it will take up valuable time and is just a whim of mine, but I thought I might devote an hour or two to it each evening for a while, just for my own satisfaction.'

'You mean stay late?'

'Yes. My wife can always put back dinner; in fact, she has so many commitments in the afternoons, bridge, sales of work, charity committees and the like. I guess a later dinner would be quite acceptable to her.'

What he could have said was that dinner-times were becoming increasingly tedious. For years he'd had to endure Jessie's pontifications about her committees and problems posed by rebel members and now this latest topic of conversation—Alex and Annabel and their scandal—made dinner-times even more of a strain. He came out of his luxury of self-pity conscious that Laura was speaking.

'Could I help you with the work, Mr Freeman? I mean, I don't have to get home early every night. We don't often eat until eight o'clock and I have no commitments outside my work.'

Soothing words. She was a treasure. Just as devoted to Freeman & Son as he was himself. Employees like Laura Collins were thin on the ground in these days of trade unions and employees' rights.

'I'd pay you overtime of course,' he said.

'Oh there's no need for that, Mr Freeman. It would be a pleasure. I have no hobbies to keep me occupied, I'm afraid.' She smiled ruefully. 'Neither do I do any good works to take up my time.'

'I'm sure you have no need to reproach yourself, Laura. You do a good job here and you look after your mother and your son. No woman could do more.'

She tucked her handbag under her arm and retreated to the door. Their eyes locked, then they smiled.

'Until tomorrow then,' he said.

'Until tomorrow, Mr Freeman,' she replied.

CHAPTER EIGHT

'I want it clearly understood,' Alex said, 'that you do not ring me again at my office.'

'You surely aren't a junior to have your calls monitored?'

'No. I'm not a junior, neither am I a senior partner, not yet at any rate, and I need to keep the respect of my colleagues.'

Rosemary pouted prettily.

'Surely a call from your future wife won't harm your precious reputation?'

'Future wife?'

'Well, aren't I?'

His mouth was grim as he replied, 'I haven't given up hope yet of saving my marriage.'

'But she's moved out.'

'So?'

'That seems to me to be pretty final.' Rosemary held out her glass. 'Fill me up again, darling please. I feel like celebrating, it's not every day I get fame as a co-respondent.'

As he lunged to her sideboard and picked up the gin bottle he said, *'If* there is a divorce, no one will be named as co-respondent. It will be a civilized divorce sought because of incompatibility. Annabel wants it that way and the least I can do is to agree.'

Rosemary's heart sank.

'You mean it isn't because of your affair with me?'

'Not entirely. That, for Annabel, was the final straw, but I see now that it's been a possibility for some time. I've been a complete bloody prat and now I'm paying for it.'

'Are you saying there have been other women?'

He shrugged. 'Annabel seems to think so.

I've tried to reason with her, to convince her that she's the only woman for me, but her sudden renewal of friendship with that bloody Pepper Finlay hasn't helped. She's stirring it, blast her. She's a right bitch.'

Rosemary was angry now.

'You didn't tell me that Annabel was the only woman for you when you were making it with *me.*'

His mouth curved in a sneer. 'Making it with you? Wasn't it a case of *mutual* making? I seem to remember you didn't need much seducing.'

'What's happening to us, Alex? I thought you loved me.' Her mouth trembled.

His voice was a shade more gentle now. 'Look, Rosie, don't build this thing up into a great romance. It was a mutual sex romp. You knew I was married and, at that time, fully intended to stay married.'

His handsome face was momentarily haggard with emotion, and he continued as if talking to himself. 'How can I have been such a bloody, selfish fool?'

She moved closer to him and tried to put her arms round him, but he shrugged her off. Then he turned to her with the ghost of a grin.

'Let's cool it for a while, eh Rosie?'

'You mean not see each other?'

He nodded. 'I've got a lot of adjusting to do. I'm not in the mood for sexual dalliance right now.'

'Sexual dalliance? How can you be so cruel,

Alex? I loved you, I *still* love you, more than ever now, and I want us to be together always. I thought you did too.' Tears filled her eyes.

He tried to repress a shudder. Spend the rest of his life with a trollop like Rosemary Wharton? Oh Christ! What a fool I've been. I had it all—marriage to a lovely, well-bred woman who would never give me a moment's anxiety, and I've thrown it all away for the town trollop.

Rosemary's voice cut in on his bitter reveries, 'I hear she's moved into a flat in Romney Place and that Pepper Finlay and David Seymour helped her to move in.'

He turned and spoke sharply, 'David Seymour?'

'Yeh. That dishy manager of the Crown Hotel.'

'What's *he* got to do with Annabel?'

Rosemary shrugged. 'Maybe he's her new man. As far as I know he's unattached and,' malicously she added, 'sexy too; *very* easy on the eye.'

Alex was furious. David Seymour! He knew the man, of course, but he'd never remotely considered him in connection with Annabel. The idea hurt, hurt like hell. He searched his mind for facts about the Crown Hotel manager but he'd never had much conversation with David Seymour. He'd seen the man about the district driving a red sports car, sometimes with a female pasenger, but mostly on his own.

Beyond a nod and casual greeting when he'd gone into the Crown, Alex had never had much to do with the man. The idea of Annabel and David Seymour was monstrous. Suspicions crowded his mind. Could this David Seymour have anything to do with Annabel's sudden desire for a divorce? When could they have met to become involved? Easily, reason said, you weren't around all the time, were you? You were too busy chasing after bimbos like Rosemary Wharton. Suddenly he wanted to get out of here, away from this clinging, common woman. He couldn't think why she'd ever attracted him in the first place.

'I have to go,' he said. 'I have matters to attend to.' He drained his drink and put the glass down on what she called her 'bar'—a shelf cluttered with glasses and bottles of booze. He thought of his own home so elegantly run by Annabel, the relaxed atmosphere, the efficient ministerings of Gwen and Frank Lovell under the gentle supervision of Annabel whom they obviously liked and admired. What sort of life would there be for him in his house now? He thought of the days before Annabel when he had led a bachelor existence using his home just as a base, never being there long enough to appreciate the comforts of a well-run home.

Rosemary sidled up to him. 'You can't go yet, Alex. I've got a meal waiting in the kitchen. I thought we'd have a quiet cosy evening together and discuss our plans for the future.'

Her heart was in her eyes as she pleaded with him. He was embarrassed and faintly ashamed, yet he told himself, he'd never led this woman to believe she'd ever be more to him than a passing romp. Besides, he wanted to get away to think over what she'd implied about Annabel and David Seymour. Could David Seymour be the reason for Annabel's sudden desire for a divorce? No, he was sure in his heart that Annabel had never been unfaithful to him, yet the poison of suspicion was working.

'I'm sorry, Rosie,' he said, 'but I have to be alone to work things out. My life's been shattered and I can't think straight at the moment.'

He picked up his briefcase and made for the door.

'Thanks for the drinks. I'll give you a ring sometime.' He attempted a grin. 'Don't take any wooden nickels, Rosie.'

Tears wet on her cheeks, she hurled at him, 'Bastard! And to think I was ready to give up everything for *you*. Go and be damned to you! There's plenty more fish in the sea. See if *I* care. You can . . .'

He closed the door on her ravings and went out to his car.

*　　*　　*

'You've got a lovely view over the marshes,'

David Seymour said.

Annabel managed a weak grin. 'Except that there's nothing to see on the marshes except the marshes.'

He grinned back at her. 'You never know. You might be the first person to spot the rare purple-breasted lesser warbler.'

'Bird-watching's never appealed to me.'

He sat down on the settee beside her.

'Me either, except when I was in my teens, then it was a different kind of bird.'

She looked at him curiously.

'David,' she said, 'snub me if I'm talking out of line, but have you never wanted to remarry?'

'I wouldn't dream of snubbing you, Annabel my dear. No, as yet, I've never had the urge to remarry.'

'I don't think I shall ever want to,' she sighed.

His eyes grew serious. 'You never know, Annabel. Time is a great healer.' He stood up. 'Now, let's get that bureau in the right place, then I'd better go. When I'm up here watching the glimmerings of spring over the marshes I tend to forget that I'm a working man.'

Annabel got up too.

'Oh David, you and Pep have been so wonderful to me. I don't know how I'd ever have got this far without the two of you. I can't tell you how grateful I am for your support and caring.'

He moved the bureau a fraction to the right before he replied, 'You don't have to be grateful. It's a pleasure. Pep loves organizing and I'm a natural dogsbody. Now, all you have to do is to concentrate on the guest list for your house-warming party.'

Annabel mustered a smile. 'Yes. I've already spoken to some of the tenants in this block. They seem very nice people. There's a retired army officer and his wife and a headmistress of a girls' school, they're on the floor below me, then at the top there's the writer, Joe Linden. I passed him on the stairs and said "Hello", but he looked a bit sour. Still, I'll invite him just the same.' She gave a little giggle. 'Maybe as he's a celebrity he thought I had a nerve to speak to him.'

David frowned. 'Didn't he reply to your "hello"?'

'He nodded, but he didn't speak or smile.'

'He's reputed to be somewhat of a hell raiser,' David said. 'No stranger to divorce, I hear.'

'Oh,' said Annabel, attempting flippancy. 'Maybe he can give me some pointers then if he's had all that much experience of divorce.'

David was silent. Cynical flippancy didn't suit Annabel. He hoped she wouldn't become hard like Pepper, but her next remark reassured him.

'Oh David, I wonder if I'll ever get used to being a divorcee? Sometimes in the night when

I can't sleep I ask myself if the breakdown of my marriage is my fault. I feel I may have failed Alex in some way.'

'You haven't failed him, Annabel,' David said gently. 'Rest assured, you haven't failed him.'

She smiled at him and he realized, with surprise, that he'd like to kiss her.

'Thank you David,' she said. 'You are so very kind.'

*   *   *

Laura Collins waited whilst Albert Freeman locked the outside door of the store. He looked at his watch.

'Just half past seven. It's amazing how much work we've got through, Laura, since five-thirty. I feel terrible about taking up your leisure time like this.'

She smiled at him. 'I can honestly say, Mr Freeman, that I've loved every minute of it. I think probably because it's not my routine work—it's kind of a fun thing.' Her eyes clouded. 'Oh, that sounds silly, doesn't it? I'm not very good with words I'm afraid, I . . .'

He cut in on her, 'I know exactly what you mean, Laura. It's the same for me. And, in addition,' he added in his usual pompous style, 'it's proved me right. There *was* a fraction more profit in the old lines so despised by today's customers—blouses, skirts, frocks . . .' He

81

stopped and grinned weakly. 'I'm told by my wife that I mustn't use that word "frock". The word is "dress" nowadays. "Frock" is old hat so Jessie says.'

Sedately Laura walked by him to the car.

'Your wife sounds very with it Mr Freeman.'

He slowed a minute and looked at her.

'With it? Jessie? No, I wouldn't say Jessie was all that modern. She's inclined to stick with the old styles and old customs,' and, he thought, those deadly old clichés she's inherited from her mother.

'Jessie has quotes for everything,' he said now to Laura, 'you know, "a stitch in time" sort of thing.'

'She always looks very smart, Mr Freeman.'

'Yes. I suppose she does.'

But Albert didn't want to talk about Jessie. He wanted to savour every precious minute with this amazing young woman who had suddenly brought something like light into his humdrum life. He opened his car door and ushered her into the passenger seat.

'Now, I suppose, Laura, you'll go home and start work all over again preparing the evening meal for yourself and your mother.'

'Oh, it won't take long, Mr Freeman. I did all the vegetables this morning before I left for work.'

'You make me feel ashamed. *My* meal will be ready for me when I get in.'

She smiled at him as she fastened her seat

belt.

'Oh, I'm not complaining. I'm a very lucky woman, really. I have a nice home and a job I love. What more could one ask?'

He looked at her and thought how nice it was to have her here beside him. He wished he could take her out for a meal to round off a pleasant evening, but he knew it was quite out of the question. Maybe he could give her a small present, a reward for the overtime she was giving him, but it was a delicate situation. He would have to give it more thought.

Before he started the car he said, 'Did you really mean it when you said you loved your job, Laura?'

'Yes, Mr Freeman. I really and truly love my job.'

He started the car.

'Then I'm a very lucky man, Laura, a very lucky man.'

Almost to herself Laura murmured, 'People say if you live between the sea and the canal, like I do, you're in the evil belt, but I've never believed it, and I believe it even less now.' She sighed blissfully.

In her flat opposite, over the charity shop, old Peggy Lambert watched them drive away.

She muttered as she settled one of her cats on her lap, a crafty smile playing over her mouth, 'Once, yes, Tiddliwinks my precious.' She stroked the cat's head. 'Once yes, but twice, Tiddliwinks, decidedly fishy.'

83

CHAPTER NINE

'Looking out to sea can be very lonely when one lives alone,' the estate agent had told her. 'Wouldn't you be better off, Mrs Clifton, in a property with an inland outlook—people and buildings around you?'

But she had wanted this flat so she had ignored his advice. Now she was beginning to appreciate the truth of his words. Looking out to sea *was* lonely. She stepped back from the balcony into the sitting-room. Tomorrow was the 1st of March—spring would soon be here—time to begin a new life.

Her apartment was on the middle floor. The block consisted of six flats, two on each floor. The six apartments were all big, consisting of a spacious sitting-room, equally roomy dining-room, a fair-sized kitchen, two large bedrooms and a luxurious bathroom with separate shower cubicle and lavatory, with, what was unusual in modern flats, huge cupboards and built-in wardrobes. The other flat on Annabel's floor was occupied by the widow of a doctor, a pretty woman in her mid-fifties, Dorothy Barber. Annabel had spoken to her briefly when they'd met on the stairs.

On the top floor, next to Joe Lindon, the writer, was an apartment occupied by a young girl named Tracy Atkins who worked in a florist's shop in Copmarsh. Annabel had seen the girl parking her car in the garage allotted to her in the courtyard below, but had not, as yet, spoken to her. She was an intense-looking brunette and, each time Annabel had seen her, the girl had appeared to be in a hurry. Idly Annabel wondered if the girl had any contact with her neighbour on the top floor—the dour writer, Joe Linden.

One of the flats on the ground floor was occupied by a retired colonel, Ivor Ramsay, and his wife, Jean. In the flat next to them lived a forty-nine-year-old spinster named Miranda Phillips, headmistress of a girls' school.

Well, Annabel decided, she would invite all the residents of the flats to her house-warming party and take it from there. She had no desire to start serious relationships with any of them, but she knew she would have to find something to occupy her time and mind with no husband now to share her life. Maybe she should get a job, but she certainly didn't need the money and didn't think she'd take kindly to being tied. Charity works like that undertaken by her sister held no appeal for her. She would gladly donate to good causes, but she had no desire to work for them.

She thought back to the days before her marriage. Time hadn't been heavy on her hands then, so why should it be now? Because I've let my life revolve around Alex, she decided. Maybe things would have worked out better for us if I'd had a career or some outside interest. But, reason said, that wouldn't have prevented his infidelity. No, as a wife I've obviously been a failure. Jess was so right when she predicted that our marriage wouldn't work. Jess was so like Mum, always right about things. Why couldn't I have been more like Jess? Then she laughed silently; if I had been, I certainly wouldn't have attracted Alex. The idea of Alex married to a woman like Jess was ludicrous. Just as the idea of me being married to pompous Albert, she thought with wry amusement, was equally unthinkable.

Her musings were cut short by a loud ringing of the doorbell. Surprised she went to answer it. A young man in a track suit held out to her an enormous arrangement of flowers, so large that they almost hid his face. From behind the blossoms he said, 'You are Mrs Clifton?'

'Yes.'

'Then these are for you,' and he thrust the huge arrangement of flowers into her arms. Over the top of them she looked at him.

'Thank you. I wasn't expecting . . .'

He cut in on her. 'Just moved in 'ave yer?'

'Yes. That's right.'

He grinned. 'Nice flats these. Wasn't so long ago that this ground had the old fishin' sheds on it. Real grotty it was then.'

Annabel smiled back at him.

'Yes. I remember. I didn't think then that

86

I'd be living here.'

He started to move away. 'No. Never know what's waitin' for yer round the corner, do yer? That's what me mum always says.'

'And she's right,' Annabel replied. 'Thank you so much.'

He gave her a wave as he went to the top of the stairs.

'Good luck, ma'am. Be 'appy.'

Be happy she thought wryly as she extricated the gift card from the flowers. At first she thought they might have come from Jess and Albert, but it wasn't their style. No, she should have known. 'Lots of happy fun times, love from Pepper and David'.

She took the flowers through to the kitchen. It would take her ages to arrange them, but first she must ring Pepper and David to thank them. Ah well, she consoled herself, that takes care of the morning. This afternoon I'll write my invitations to my house-warming after I've fixed a date with Pepper because the Crown Hotel will be doing the catering. At least now I won't have to spend the day reading or staring out at the bleak sea, she consoled herself. Tomorrow I must sort out some way of spending my days so that I don't brood and become bitter.

Taking up golf, bridge or bowls held no appeal for her, but there was always her old schoolfriend, Sally Soames, owner of a small exclusive gown shop in the High Street. She knew she could drift in and out assisting Sally with her paperwork or giving advice to Sally's customers, most of whom were known to her. She knew that Sally couldn't afford to pay a full-time assistant so, she decided, as well as being occupational therapy for herself, it would also help Sally. She had, on occasion, helped Sally by modelling some of the garments for customers, most of whom were also schoolfriends of them both.

In the midst of her musings the telephone rang. She answered it to her solicitor, James Botham.

'I've had several calls from Alex,' he told her, 'asking if I can arrange a reconciliation.'

'Oh, I'm so sorry he's been taking that line,' said Annabel. 'I told him there's absolutely no chance of us staying together and that I wanted a divorce to go through as quickly and painlessly as possible.'

'Yes. I told him it was unethical and that it was no good trying to change things. I think he's finally got the message, but I did think, Annabel, that I ought to let you know about his calls, just in case you might have had second thoughts about it.'

'No,' said Annabel firmly. 'It's far too late now for that. I'm starting a new life here and I want to get the divorce over with. After all, we're both civilized people, so it should be possible to get the thing done with dignity.'

'Yes. I'm sure you're right,' he said, 'but I did

88

feel I ought to tell you that Alex was still clutching at straws and that I'm making this call as a family friend, Annabel, and not as a lawyer.'

'Yes. I appreciate that, James, but I'm afraid it's too late.'

When she had replaced the receiver Annabel set about finding vases for her flowers. The evening's television programmes were quite good, so that would take care of the hours after dinner. She had declined Pepper's offer to dine at the Crown, saying that she had to start getting used to being alone. Also, Jess had tentatively suggested that she might like to dine with her and Albert, but she had declined that invitation too. Listening to Jess and Albert pontificating in their smug domestic security was the last thing she wanted.

Before arranging the flowers she rang the Crown Hotel and, after giving her name, asked to speak to Mrs Finlay. She waited and eventually a man's voice came through to her.

'It's David here, Annabel. Sorry but Pep is out. Can I help you or take a message for her?'

'You've already helped me, David. I'm just ringing to say thank you to you and Pep for the wonderful flowers. They are simply lovely.'

'We thought they'd bring a bit of cheer into your new home.'

'They've certainly done that. I thank you so much and will you please thank Pepper for me?'

'I certainly will. She's over at the fishing sheds getting supplies. Would you like her to call you when she gets back?'

'Not really. I only rang to say a big thank you for the flowers. I mustn't take up your time, David, I know how busy you are.'

'Never too busy to talk to you, Annabel.'

Annabel was embarrassed. There was a warmth in his voice that worried her slightly. Then she told herself not to be so stupid. She was vulnerable and that was probably the reason for her silly fancies.

'Goodbye then, David, and thanks once again.'

'Goodbye, Annabel. Take care.'

Just half an hour later Pepper rang.

'Sorry I was out when you called, Annie. I was over the marshes getting the fish. There's one young fisherman trading there who really gives me the hots and makes me wish I was nineteen and innocent.'

'Pep, you're terrible,' Annabel laughed. 'It was sweet of you and David to send me the lovely flowers. They must have cost a fortune.'

'Glad you liked them, love. Listen, I'm ringing because I heard a bit of news in town today that I thought might interest you.'

'Don't tell me: Jess has eloped with the vicar.'

'No. Nothing to do with Jess. It's about that woman Alex has been fooling with, the cow from the antiques shop.'

'Rosemary Wharton?'

'Yes. Her assistant told Mandy Cane in the charity shop that Alex seems to have ditched her.'

Annabel was silent a moment, digesting the news. Then she said calmly, 'I always thought he would as soon as he knew he was free to have her. She's just not his style.'

'And it doesn't make any difference to you? You're still going ahead with the divorce?'

'Of course. If I go back now, the same thing will happen again. It won't be long before there's another Rosemary Wharton. Besides, I've just given James Botham the go-ahead. Changing the subject, Pep, would next Saturday week be all right with you for my house-warming party? You did say your people would do the food for me.'

'Yes. That's fine. Tell me, were you serious when you said you'd invite Alex?'

Annabel was silent a moment, then she said, 'No. That was just bravado. I couldn't possibly invite Alex. It would be a cheap and tasteless gesture.'

'Yes. I guess you're right. Now, how are you settling in?'

'It'll take a bit of getting used to, but I'll survive. I thought I might help Sally Soames in her gown shop when I have time on my hands. I helped her in the past before I was married.'

Pepper was enthusiastic.

'That's a super idea. And don't forget I'm

always here if you need someone to talk to, or drink with.'

'I know, Pep, and I'm more than grateful. You've been wonderful to me, you *and* David.'

'Well, we've both been there, pet, so we know how to cope with the fall-out.'

'Yes. Thanks again, Pep. I'm going to get my invites out now and I'll let you know as soon as possible how many people I think will be coming to my house-warming.'

'Cheers and don't hesitate to ring us if you need anything or even if you just want to talk. Uncle David and Auntie Pep are always at your service.'

'Thanks Pep. You're a tonic. Goodbye.'

*   *   *

He came swiftly round a bend in the stairs and almost cannoned into her. She stepped back to lean against the wall.

'Sorry,' he said curtly. 'I'm not used to seeing people on the stairs. Most of 'em on the top two floors use the lift.'

She studied him briefly before she replied. His shirt was open at the neck and he looked as if he needed a shave, but there was a pleasant drift of an expensive body lotion around him.

'I'm sorry,' she said, 'but I have claustrophobia in lifts.'

'Well, this one *has* been known to get stuck,' he said, 'and it's a bloody waste of time cooped

92

up in it waiting . . .'

She shuddered. 'Oh, how awful! Then I shall certainly not be using it. I'd be terrified shut in such a small space. I . . .'

Rudely he cut in on her, 'There's no danger. Colonel Ramsay on the ground floor usually gets it going eventually.' He grinned nastily, 'If he's in, of course.'

He started to move away.

'Mr Linden. That *is* your name, isn't it?' Without waiting for his reply she rushed on, 'I'm Annabel Clifton. I've just moved into Flat 3 and I'm having a small house-warming party next Saturday week. I'd be delighted if you'd come. Around eight. I *was* going to write proper invitations but . . .'

Before she could finish he cut in on her again, 'I'm not a party man.'

'It won't exactly be a party. More of an introduction for me to other residents.'

His eyes raked her with unconcealed insolence.

'Oh, there's not much to know about the other residents. They don't fight or indulge in drunken orgies, not in public anyway.'

She was really annoyed now.

'I didn't suppose they did, but I thought it would be a friendly gesture. Please don't bother to come if you think it's a stupid idea.'

He smiled then and, in spite of his uncouth appearance, she found herself responding to the magnetism of the man.

'I'll look in then if I'm free that night, but if the other residents have told you in the meantime what a sod I am, I won't hold it against you if you shut the door in my face.'

He flashed her a grin which, just for a second, made him look quite young, then he moved away and ran down the stairs.

She stayed where she was for a few seconds, then made her way leisurely down the stairs. As she walked slowly into town she wondered if she had been wise to decide so quickly on where to live now that she was on her own.

A pale yellowy sun was parting the clouds and a few children were playing on the parkland opposite the flats. All the buildings in the short road were fairly new and in pristine condition. If this *is* the evil belt, she thought, it doesn't look very forbidding today. As she walked she grew more cheerful. Yes, I do think I did the right thing in deciding to live here. I've only myself to think of now, so it's up to me to make it work. She grinned to herself as she thought of Jess. 'As ye sow so shall ye reap', eh Jess? So I've done the sowing, now for the reaping.

Strangely it was not Alex she was thinking of as she sauntered along the road, but of the two men who had so recently catapulted into her life—David Seymour and Joe Linden. Two very different men, but both with one thing in common, what she had hitherto only seen in her husband—animal magnetism. She realized with a shock that, since her marriage, she had never really seen any other man but Alex.

There was a faint smile on her lips and a new light in her eyes as she walked steadily on into town.

CHAPTER TEN

'I think it's in extremely bad taste,' said Jessie. 'It's flaunting herself almost. I hate to think what Mumma would have felt about such a tasteless action.'

'Is it such a dreadful thing,' Albert ventured, 'for Annabel to gather a few friends together to see her new home?'

Jessie glared at him.

'I guess it's that awful Pepper Finlay at the back of it. Well, I for one, won't be there.'

Albert sipped his sherry before replying, then he said mildly, 'I think you should be, Jess. Take it as a cry for help. She needs your support. After all, you *are* her only close relative.'

An idea was slowly shaping in his mind, but Jessie's next remark brought him down to earth.

'The invitation includes you as well, Albert. I wouldn't go without you.'

The flaring idea in his mind wilted and died.

'I shan't go, Jess. Consider my position in the

town. I don't want to be seen as condoning the breakdown of a marriage.'

Jessie stared at him, her chin quivering with annoyance.

'Yet you expect me to go. Really, Albert, I don't know what's come over you lately. Sometimes I think I don't really know you. Well, I certainly wouldn't go without you. The invitation is for both of us.'

'I could plead pressure of work. I would drop you off, say "hello" to Annabel,' he smiled gently, 'even have a little drink with her to wish her well in her new home, then pick you up a couple of hours later.'

Jessie couldn't believe her ears. Albert's behaviour lately seemed to get more and more strange—unless it's me, she thought, am I having silly middle-age fancies?'

'I couldn't possibly agree to that,' she snapped, 'and what would you be doing whilst I was at Annabel's?'

'My dear, I have a load of paperwork to catch up with at the store. I assure you, I would be quite happy working away on my books with the store closed and quiet. I could get sandwiches from the new sandwich bar two doors down the High Street. After all, it won't hurt me to have a light evening meal for a change. And those sandwiches look very substantial.' He smiled. 'I know that some of my staff patronize that shop daily, saves them having to bring food from home or going out to expensive restaurants. Presumably Annabel will provide adequate food for her party guests. After all, it does say a buffet party so you should be able to get plenty to eat, fancy stuff too, I'll be bound. Knowing Annabel.'

Jessie was really put out now. After all these years of marriage she thought she knew Albert as well as she knew herself but, just lately, he seemed to have changed. Could it be the male menopause, she wondered, but inwardly she shuddered. Her fastidious soul shied away from what she called 'dirty thoughts'.

'No, I definitely shall not go to the party without you.' She stared at him as if seeing him for the first time. 'I might have considered it if you had agreed to go too. No, I shall show Annabel my displeasure by boycotting her party. I think it's in extremely bad taste, anyway.'

Albert's hopes died. He had contemplated sandwiches for himself and Laura, washed down with a full-blooded red wine, whilst they went through their work. Laura had indicated that she would be willing to put in a few hours over a weekend if he wished, and he had already earmarked a pretty flowered housecoat to give to her the next time they were alone together. She refused to accept overtime money, but she would surely accept a carefully chosen gift to show his appreciation of her loyalty to the store. In his books he would record the housecoat as a gift to a local charity to satisfy the auditors. Jessie's next words cut into his melancholy musings.

'Is anything wrong at the store, Albert?'

He was startled by the sharpness of her voice.

'Of course not, Jess. What makes you ask that?'

'It's just that you seem . . .'

'Seem what?'

She twisted her hands together and he noticed how plump and yellow they were in contrast to Laura's pale elegant hands.

'Not your usual self. You used to stand by me no matter what . . .' Her lips trembled and he was afraid she was going to cry. He moved over to her and put an arm round her shoulders.

'What makes you think I'm not standing by you, Jess? What have I done?'

She moved out of his embrace and tidied the fussy lace mat on the centre of the sitting-room table.

'You don't seem to bother about the disgrace Annabel has brought on us as much as I'd have thought you would.'

He mustered a weak smile.

'It's not Annabel who has brought the disgrace, Jess. As I see it, it's Alex.'

She gazed at him appealingly.

'But Annabel is acting so . . . so . . .'

'So what?'

'Well, I don't know exactly. The way that Pepper Finlay would act, I suppose, as if she was almost enjoying the breakdown of her marriage. Oh, I wish Mumma were still alive—she'd know what to do.'

'My dear Jess,' said Albert gently, 'I don't think anything your dear mama could have said or done would have any effect on Annabel. She disregarded our advice when she married Alex Clifton and I don't think anyone could make her change her mind once it's made up.' More gently now he added, 'She's not a caring, dutiful person like you, Jess.'

'Oh Albert.'

She came willingly into his arms now.

'Don't ever fail me, Albert, please.'

Albert was surprised at this uncharacteristic behaviour of his wife.

'Of course I won't fail you, Jess. Whatever brought this on?'

'I don't know.' She pulled away from him and stroked the top of her chest.

'It's just that, lately, I've had funny sharp pains up here. I'm sure it's all this worry over Annabel.'

'Quite probably,' said Albert soothingly. 'But if you're worried, Jess, go and see Dr Willard.'

'Oh, it's not that bad.'

'Even so . . .'

She smiled weakly. 'All right, if it gets any worse I'll go and see him. Well, I must go and dish up. Maisie's surpassed herself tonight, the pheasant is cooked just the way you like it. I've let her go off early. I told her we could manage.'

Albert smiled, relieved that Jess seemed to have reverted to her normal self.

'The pheasant season is over now, I suppose,' he said, 'so we must make the best of this last one. I'm not keen on too much frozen stuff.'

Jessie smiled back at him. She told herself her silly fears were all part of the change of life, like the pains in her upper chest. Albert was the same as always and she was stupid to doubt him. I'd die if I lost Albert, she thought suddenly, but his hand on her shoulder as they went into the dining-room reassured her. All was right in her world in spite of Annabel and her silly new image.

*   *   *

Sally Soames draped a dress over a hanger as she smiled at her friend.

'A party, Annabel? What a super idea. May I bring a friend?'

'Of course. Male or female?'

'Male I'm afraid.'

'Don't be afraid. I was thinking males will be a bit thin on the floor so the more the merrier. Who is he? Anyone I know?'

'No. A fabric traveller. Married I'm afraid, but if he's to be believed, about to break up with his wife.' She smiled ruefully. 'But then, that's the story of my life. I've heard it all before many times.'

'Well, bring him to the party anyway,' said Annabel, 'and we'll take it from there. I heard today that the former owner of my flat left Copmarsh to get married for the second time and is delirously happy, so maybe there's hope for me even though I do live in the so-called evil belt.'

Sally regarded her seriously.

'Would you like to get married again, Annabel?'

Images of David Seymour and Joe Linden leapt unbidden into Annabel's thoughts and she was angry at the intrusion.

'No,' she said firmly. 'Definitely not. I aim to have fun now with none of the tedious ties of marriage.'

When she'd finished her errands in the town she walked along to Hawthorn Avenue where Jessie and Albert lived. It was a tree-lined avenue with six large houses in it. Annabel smiled to herself as she caught glimpses of the canal between the houses. No way would Jessie ever have agreed to live between the sea and the canal, the reputed evil belt, and although the canal could be seen clearly from Jessie's back garden, Jessie and Albert were safely on the town side of the two waters. She walked up the short drive to her sister's front door, marvelling as always at the immaculate front garden, the neat borders sporting the spring crocuses and the red brick path leading to the front door swept and shining. A few dead leaves were sticking to the imposing name board attached to the porch pillars—Hawthorn Lodge. Annabel removed the offending leaves with her gloved hand and grimaced as the wet seeped through the fabric on to her hand. She rang the doorbell and it was immediately answered by Maisie Webb—Jessie's maid and general factotum.

'Good morning, Mrs Clifton.'

'Good morning, Maisie. Is my sister in?'

Jessie moved up behind the maid.

'Yes, Annabel, I am. Come in quickly out of the cold.'

Smiling, Maisie Webb stepped back to allow Annabel room to move into the spacious hall.

'Coffee in the morning-room, Maisie please,' said Jessie and, to Annabel, 'when will this winter end? It's still very cold.'

'Oh, I thought it was a shade warmer today,' said Annabel. She peered at her sister. 'You look pale, Jess. Are you all right?'

Jessie looked round to make sure the maid was on her way to the kitchen before she replied. Then, ushering Annabel into the morning-room and lowering her voice she said, 'I think I'm all right, Annabel, except that I have funny sharp pains in the upper part of my chest. Not all the time, just occasional bouts.'

Annabel looked at her anxiously.

'Have you seen Dr Willard?'

102

'No.' Jessie ushered her sister into an armchair by the window. 'It's not bad enough to bother Dr Willard with. It's most likely to be indigestion and . . .' her voice took on the familiar censorious note Annabel knew so well, 'and, of course, there's all the worry of you and Alex.'

Annabel leant back in her chair and, with a sigh of frustration, she said, 'Really, Jess. Can't you get it into your head that this divorce of mine has nothing to do with you and Albert?'

'Of course it has,' said Jessie, 'you're my only close relative next to Albert and people will think it's my duty to stop you from wrecking your life.'

Annabel leant forward in her chair.

'Look, Jess, what I do cannot be blamed on you or Albert. As for wrecking my life, as you so dramatically put it, on the contrary, I feel as if my life is just beginning. I'm meeting new people, and I know the pitfalls now, so I'm well prepared to cope. Now . . .' her voice dropped a tone, 'I've come here today, Jess, to try to change your mind about coming to my house-warming party.'

Jessie's mouth drooped. 'We think, Annabel, that it is in very bad taste.'

'Why should it be? Most people have a house-warming party when they move into a new house.'

'But not . . . not . . .' Jess floundered, at a loss for words.

103

'Not gay divorcees? Why not, Jess? Why shouldn't I welcome new friends into my new home? Alex is the guilty party, not me.'

Jessie struggled to find the right words.

'It's just that, it seems ... well...' she finally blurted out, 'It's in very bad taste. It's almost as if you're, well, celebrating ...'

Annabel smiled. 'Well, so I am. I'm celebrating my new life and my new friends. There are some intesting people in my block of flats. There's a sultry young beauty called Tracy Atkins, works at the florist's, and, on her floor there is the writer, Joe Linden. He spoke to me briefly on the stairs the other day.'

Jessie frowned. 'You must be careful of him, Annabel. He has a bad reputation. I hear that his books contain obscene language. In fact, Miss Briggs at the library says they are downright filthy, and he's been married several times I hear.'

'Well, I've asked him to my party,' said Annabel lightly. 'But I promise I won't ask him to do a reading from one of his books.' Seeing her sister's look of disapproval, she laughed and went on quickly, 'Now, my ground-floor neighbours are very different, eminently respectable, a Colonel Ramsay and his wife and a headmistress of a girls' school—Miss Miranda Phillips.'

'We know Miranda Phillips,' said Jessie primly. 'She's a very clever woman, granddaughter of a dean, I believe.'

'Well, there you are,' said Annabel lightly. 'At least I have *some* respectable neighbours and they're all invited to my party, so you'd be in good company. Jess, please change your mind and come.'

The mention of Miranda Phillips had impressed Jessie. The pain in her chest was flaring again now. Involuntarily she put up a hand to stroke herself. Annabel noticed and said quickly, 'What's the matter, Jess? Are you in pain?'

Jessie quickly dropped her hand.

'No. It's nothing. Just a spasm. Feels like indigestion. Now, about your party, Annabel, are you sure Colonel Ramsay and Miss Phillips are coming?'

'Well, I haven't had their replies yet,' admitted Annabel, 'but I put the invites in their letter boxes and they always speak to me when we meet so I'm hoping they'll come.'

'Well, I'll mention it to Albert again,' said Jessie, 'but he did say definitely that he couldn't go.'

'Couldn't or wouldn't?'

'I don't question Albert's motives,' said Jessie stiffly. 'And I think that if more women had respect for their husband's wishes there'd be fewer divorces.'

'Even if the husband's wish was to bed another woman?' asked Annabel flippantly.

Jessie flashed her a look of distaste.

'Really, Annabel, you've got very coarse

105

since you've renewed your friendship with Pepper Finlay.' She gave a little snort. 'Stupid name, Pepper.'

'Pep has been my lifeline,' said Annabel soberly. 'She understands.'

'And I don't I suppose?' said Jessie bitterly. To her own surprise she was nearly in tears. What's the matter with me lately, she asked herself, letting things get to me like this? Firstly, Albert seems strange, almost indifferent to my problems, now Annabel is behaving like a hostile rebellious child. The pain flared up again and her heart cried out to the woman long gone who had coped with all family problems. Oh, Mumma, why did you have to die? You'd have known exactly what to do.

'Cream or milk?' she asked her sister as the maid placed the coffee tray on the table.

CHAPTER ELEVEN

Joe Linden glanced briefly at the girl curled up on his bed before stepping into his jeans. He adjusted the belt and mooched over to the dressing-table to pick up a pack of cigarettes. She watched him with sullen eyes.

'So what do you think of her then?'

'Who?'

'The ladybird on the middle floor.'

'Do I have to think of her?'

'She was one of the rich Stantons, used to own breweries.'

'So?'

'I heard she's split up with her husband, the dishy Alex Clifton.'

He made no answer, just picked up some papers from his dressing-table and put them on a chair.

'I have work to do, infant.' He put on an exaggerated accent. 'And I want to be alone.'

Leisurely she swung her legs round and got up from the bed.

'In other words, scram.'

'You said it, sweetheart.'

She moved over to him, removed the cigarette from his lips, took it in her mouth, gave a little draw on it, then put it back in his mouth again.

'I'm cooking a curry tonight. Want to come in for some?'

He went over and smoothed the crumpled bedclothes.

'No thanks. I want to work.'

'But you've got to eat.'

'Who says so?'

She stared at him as she got dressed.

'Are you gonna make it with her, Joe?'

'Make what with who?'

'You know damn well who. The bimbo who's just moved in on the middle floor.'

He frowned. 'I don't think she's a bimbo.'

'Oh.' Tracy Atkins was on the defensive now,

but she knew better than to bombard this man with intimacies.

'I've had a written invite to her house-warming party next Saturday,' she told him.

'Oh, and are you going?'

'I don't know. Did you get an invite?'

'Not a written one.'

Her voice was sharp. 'But you *did* get one?'

He grinned as he picked up her handbag and tossed it to her. 'We met on the stairs. She mentioned it then.'

'You never said.'

He shrugged. 'Did I have to?'

'Are you going?'

Again a shrug.

Eagerly she said, 'We could go together if you like.'

She was fully dressed now and he took her arm and led her to the door.

'Scram, infant. I want to work.'

'You didn't answer my question.'

'And what question was that?'

'Could we go to this woman's party together?'

As he opened the door he said quietly, 'You make your own arrangements. I don't know what I'm doing from one day to the next.'

'It wouldn't hurt you to go to this party with me.'

Gently he pushed her out on to the landing.

'Joe . . .'

'Goodbye Trace. Don't take any wooden

nickels.'

He closed the door on her and, fuming, she went into her flat and slammed the door.

Downstairs on the next floor Annabel put the party acceptances on the dresser. They were from Colonel Ramsay and his wife, Miranda Phillips, and Dorothy Barber, the widow on Annabel's own floor. As yet she'd had no reply from the girl, Tracy Atkins. She hadn't sent a written invitation to Joe Linden, following their brief conversation on the stairs, so she didn't expect a formal reply to the verbal invitation she'd given to him at their brief encounter.

She was dining tonight at the Crown with Pepper and David and, as she showered, she wondered if she was being wise in seeing so much of them. She had to start some time leading a lonely life and the sooner she got used to it the better. She wondered what Alex was doing tonight. She was pretty sure he wouldn't be spending the evening alone, although Pepper had heard that his affair with Rosemary Wharton had ended. The news gave Annabel no joy. She knew that if she had stayed with Alex there would always be women like Rosemary Wharton in his life. She had made a big mistake. Now she had to live with it.

*   *   *

It was two days before Annabel's house-warming party. March had come in with rolling

109

seas and cold blustery winds and Albert Freeman gently pulled up the collar of Laura Collins's coat as she waited on the pavement whilst he locked the door of the store. He was as excited as a schoolboy playing truant. He and Laura had worked for an hour on the store records and now they were going to enjoy what he called a deserved reward for hard work. Jessie had agreed to spend the evening at the local WI supper for the town's poorer pensioners and Albert had promised to get something to eat in the town.

'I can easily arrange for something to be left for you, love,' she'd told him. 'It can be kept warm in the oven.' But Albert had thanked her and declined saying that he would welcome the chance to do a spot of checking at the store after it was closed and that he would get something to eat on the way home, either in the Conservative Club or a restaurant.

'But you're not used to fast food,' Jessie had protested. 'And you know you don't care for the town's restaurants. I don't like to think of you not having a proper dinner. Maybe I'll tell them I can't help at the WI supper this year.'

'No Jessie. You mustn't do that. They rely so much on you,' he'd told her. Other years she'd left food for Albert at home, but this year he was quite adamant, saying it would be much easier for him to get a bite on the way home. As for Albert, tonight he was going to do what he had longed to do ever since discovering his

110

interest in Laura Collins. He was going to take her out to eat, somewhere far enough out of town to avoid creating any gossip. He had heard of a pub way out on the marshes which advertised food. He had made a quick trip out to inspect the small dining-room and it was empty. Also, the owners of the pub which was called The Ugly Duckling, were newcomers to the district and obviously didn't know who he was when he went in for a small sherry. He had asked if it was necessary to book for dinner and was told that, during the week, the dining-room was hardly ever used.

'Our trade is Saturday night and Sunday lunchtimes, sir,' the owner had told him, 'and then they's mostly folk in from the towns. The locals don't turn out to eat in the winter, but we're hoping for better results when it gets to spring and summer. Dead quiet it is at present, sir, no food trade to speak of, but we plod on.'

So Albert was pleased as he helped Laura into the car.

'So, your mother's meal is being taken care of tonight, Laura?'

'Yes,' she said. 'I cooked it last night. It only needs heating up. I invited Mrs Logan from next door to come in and share it with her.' She gave a little giggle. 'I'm afraid I told a fib. I said I had some urgent work to do at the store for the auditors and that I would get some food in from the sandwich bar.'

Greatly daring Albert put a hand on her

knee before he started the car.

'You don't know what this means to me, Laura, having you to myself like this, being able to take you out. I wish it didn't have to be so hole-and-corner.'

'Oh Mr Freeman,' she said excitedly. 'It's lovely. I feel like a naughty schoolgirl, like I used to feel at school when I'd done something I shouldn't.'

He leant closer to her and savoured the sweet scent she had sprayed behind her ears before leaving the store.

'I'm sure you were never a naughty schoolgirl, Laura.' Although the vision of her in a gym slip excited his imagination.

'Oh, Mr Freeman, I'm afraid I was, sometimes.'

'Laura,' he said. 'Don't you think you might call me Albert? When we're alone together I mean,' he added hastily. It would never do if she called him Albert in the store, but then, he consoled himself, she was far too sensible to do that. He was sure she was enjoying this new exciting intimacy as much as he was.

'Do you know Laura,' he said, as he drove away from the store, 'I feel like a young man going on his first date.'

She snuggled closer to him as he drove.

'I know Mr ... Albert ... I feel ever so excited, too. Really wicked. Yet all we're going to do is to have a little meal together.'

'Yes Laura.' He tried to quell his mounting

excitement and concentrate on his driving. 'Just a little meal together, that's all.'

Peggy Lambert, in her flat over the charity shop, deposited the two cats she had been nursing on to the floor. Then she got up and went over to the phone.

'Is that you Janey? Are you alone?' A cunning smile wreathed her thin mouth. 'Listen Janey. Have I got something to tell *you* about holy Joe Albie Freeman. You'll never guess what I've just seen? No, I'm not telling you over the phone. Had yer supper yet?' She waited, listening, then she said, 'Come round, will yer? Call in at the chippy on the way, my treat, then I'll tell you over supper and a mouthful of Guinness. Yeh. OK. Get skate fer me if they've got it, if not, cod'll do and a small portion of chips. Yeh. See yer.'

She sat down again and patted her lap for one of the cats to jump up.

'Well, well, Tiddliwinks, as me old dad used ter say, the things you see when you ain't got yer gun.'

CHAPTER TWELVE

As Jessie Freeman went out to get her car a sharp pain flared across her chest. She stopped for a moment, leaning against the garage door, until it died away, then she went into the garage. It's stress, she told herself. Annabel's behaviour lately had caused her so much distress and Albert hadn't been as supportive as usual. She worried that something might be wrong at the store, something he wasn't telling her about. She'd tried ringing there a little while ago, but there had been no reply. Ah well, she consoled herself, he was probably along the street at the sandwich bar and her call wasn't all that important anyway. She had only been going to suggest to him that she took a taxi to the WI supper and that he should come on there when he'd finished at the store to drive her home.

She'd decided not to stay any later than necessary at the supper, after all, she'd already done more than her share of the work in organizing it and arranging for the food. She was feeling very tired and these spasmodic pains were getting her down. If they hadn't stopped by the end of the week she would go and see Dr Willard. She'd suggest that Albert went for a check up too. He hadn't seemed himself lately. Maybe he was working too hard and maybe he cared more about Annabel's scandalous behaviour than he would admit. Probably he was playing it low-key to try to spare her pain. Just the sort of thing Albert *would* do. He was a dear man was her Albert, so steady, so supportive, and, what was very rare these days, a good Christian.

As they ate their fish and chips Janey Evans and Peggy Lambert discussed Albert Freeman's strange behaviour.

'I can't believe he's havin' an affair,' said Janey. 'He wouldn't know what to do.' She gave a coarse chuckle. 'Bet old Jessie's still a virgin.'

Peggy fed a piece of cod to one of her cats.

'Oh, I don't know. Know what they say, them what's quiet's what's 'ot.'

'Well, I'll see what Mrs Hunter-Bell thinks about it when I goes ter clean 'er place next week.'

Peggy was startled.

'You ain't gonna mention it to 'er, are yer? She's the 'ead of the WI what ol' Jessie Freeman slaves 'er guts out for.'

'Well, I think I'll just mention it, in passing like,' said Janey. 'She's a real nice woman is Mrs Hunter-B. Not stuck up at all like some of 'em at that WI. I reckon she orter know so she can put ol' Jessie wise to 'is little games.'

'Well,' said Peggy doubtfully, 'we don't ackcherly know there *are* any little games, do we?'

'Well, he don't take none of 'is other employees out in 'is car do he?'

'No,' said Peggy thoughtfully. 'Not that we know of, no 'ee don't.'

Albert restricted himself to one glass of red wine with his meal, insisting that Laura should consume the rest of the bottle.

'This drinking-driving is such a problem,' he told her.

'Well, I think it's a shame that you can't join me glass for glass.' She gave a little giggle. 'And I'm not used to all this drink. I shall probably go to sleep on the way home.'

Albert regarded her fondly and wondered again how he had overlooked her beauty over the years. She looked very desirable this evening in a pretty grey and white pleated dress, one of the more expensive dresses from the store. Her hair was in plaits coiled round her head and she was wearing a string of artificial pearls with matching ear-rings. She looked, Albert thought, the perfect lady. He noticed that the only ring she wore was the plain gold wedding band she always wore. He wished he could give her something that she could keep and wear in memory of this evening, but she had even been reluctant to accept the housecoat he'd presented her with earlier.

'Oh Mr Freeman, you shouldn't have. It's lovely, but I didn't need payment you know.'

'So, you don't like it, Laura, or you wouldn't be calling me Mr Freeman.'

'Oh . . . Albert,' she said shyly. 'I *do* like it, I love it.'

'Well then, let's say no more on the subject.'

She looked away now discreetly when he settled the bill for the meal. He glanced at his watch.

'Oh Laura,' he said, 'the evening's gone so quickly.' He noticed that it was ten o'clock and he was dismayed at the thought that Jess might have gone home already from the WI supper and might be ringing him at the store. He searched his mind for an excuse for calling in somewhere on his way home, then he thought of the verger of St Paul's Church. He could always say he'd had to pay a visit to the verger about next Sunday's services which had to embrace two christenings. Jess knew that the vicar relied on Albert to help with the organization of church affairs. His conscience pricked him just a little but, he told himself, he was a good husband to Jess, he allowed her to devote a lot of her time to the WI and her pet charities, he was surely entitled to a spot of relaxation himself.

The pub was almost empty as he and Laura said goodnight to the landlord before going out to the car. Albert was satisfied that his visit here this evening would not attract any adverse gossip locally.

Laura settled herself in the passenger seat and gave a great sigh.

He glanced down at her. 'Why the big sigh Laura?'

'Oh Mr ... Albert, it's been such a lovely

evening. I never want it to end.'

He slid an arm round her shoulders.

'I don't want it to end either.'

Before he realized what was happening she had turned and her face was close to his. The scent of her made his heart beat faster. Instinctively he gathered her closer and pressed his mouth to hers. Her urgent response startled and excited him. His hands strayed to her breasts and she gave a little moan of pleasure. With a great effort he pulled away from her.

'I'm so sorry, Laura, but you are so lovely I just couldn't help myself.'

She reached out to him.

'Oh Albert, don't stop please.'

She coiled her arms round his neck and gently he removed them.

'We mustn't, my dearest. It wouldn't be fair to you because I could never . . .'

'I know,' she interrupted him. 'I know I can never be more to you than'—she uttered a harsh little laugh—'what they call a bit on the side.'

'Oh Laura,' he said. 'Don't talk like that, please darling. You're far more to me than that, but one of us has to be strong or we won't be able to go on working together.'

She gave a little moan.

'Oh, I couldn't bear it if I didn't see you every day and I *love* my work at the store. You know I do, Albert, oh Albert . . .' She tried

118

again to reach out to him, but he took her hands, bunched them together and kissed them.

'We've got to go home, Laura. It's late. One of us has to be strong, darling.'

'Darling,' she cried. 'You called me darling. Oh, you *do* love me, Albert, don't you?'

He put her hands back in her lap and pulled her coat closer round her.

'I'm afraid I do, Laura, but sadly there's nothing I can do about it. It's not fair to you, so it would be better if you could forget tonight.'

'Oh I shall never forget it,' she said passionately. 'I love you, Albert. I think I must have loved you for a long time. Oh, Albert, don't send me away, dearest, please.'

'I shall never send you away, my darling,' said Albert gently, 'but if we are to go on seeing each other, we must try to be the way we were before we knew we were in love.'

He started the car and drove slowly out of the car-park. He glanced down at her and saw that she was crying quietly, her shoulders heaving.

'Don't cry, my darling one. Try to be happy that we are in love, even if we can't do anything about it.'

'Oh, I *am* happy, Albert. I didn't think I'd ever feel like this about anyone ever again, but I love you far more than I ever loved him— Noel's father.'

Quietly he cut in on her, 'That's music to my

ears, darling. I love you too, more than I ever thought I could love . . .'

As he spoke he thought of Jess and a stab of guilt halted him. Then he said, 'Think how lovely it will be, darling, working together every day knowing that we have our own precious secret and are hurting no one and, who knows, there may be other chances like tonight when we can steal a little happiness of our own away from the world.'

'Oh I do hope so,' she replied passionately. 'You see, Albert, I want you to love me properly one day. I think of you every night when I go to bed.'

'Oh darling, darling . . .' He forced himself to concentrate on his driving. If he stopped the car now he would be forever lost.

CHAPTER THIRTEEN

Annabel sank down in a chair by the french windows which looked out on to the canal. She had drawn back the curtains and could see the sluggish water of the canal looking, she thought, rather like a wide, yellowy-green shot-silk ribbon as the lights of the street lamps shone on it. She could hear the sea pounding against the rocks on the other side of the building. Between the sea and the canal, she thought, the belt of evil. Well, there was not much evil about tonight.

She looked round at the array of empty glasses, the remnants of the buffet dishes, the crumpled paper napkins. No one had smoked, so there was no stale smell of tobacco in the air, for which she was grateful. She supposed that the party had gone well in a dignified, subdued way, not a spectacular occasion, but not a flop either. Guests had mingled easily; the residents of the flats soon engaging in light conversation with the few from outside. Sally Soames from the gown shop was obviously known to the female residents of the flats and there had been instant rapport between them. Alas, Sally's man friend, the fabrics traveller, was a charming man, seemingly devoted to Sally but, Annabel thought, just a shade too smooth to be genuine. Still, who am I to judge, she thought. I haven't been such a great success in my choice of men.

The only guest who hadn't appeared to be at ease was the girl from the top floor—Tracy Atkins. There semed to be no camaraderie between her and the other residents of the flats and Annabel thought that perhaps she was bored with older people. Soon after she'd arrived she'd asked Annabel, 'Is Joe coming?'

'Joe?'

'Yes Joe. Joe Linden from my floor.'

Annabel shrugged. 'I wouldn't know. I invited him when I met him on the stairs recently, but he didn't seem very keen. Maybe he's wrapped up in his work. I understand he writes a lot. I must admit that I haven't read any of his books.'

'I have,' said the girl, 'and I didn't like them, but when I told him he said he didn't write for morons.'

'Charming!' said Annabel with a light laugh. 'I hope you told him what to do with his books.'

The girl had turned away and taken another drink from the maid Pepper had loaned to Annabel for the occasion. After that, Annabel didn't bother to try to cultivate the girl as it seemed obvious that she was not over-anxious to mix with the other residents of the flats. If that's the way she wants it, Annabel thought, that's fine with me. She had to admit though that she was a little disappointed that Joe Linden hadn't turned up. Although he'd hardly be tolerant of a party like this, she told herself. I can imagine that thin mouth of his curling in contempt.

In contrast, David Seymour was a decided asset to the party. Arriving early with Pepper and the maid he'd been a tower of strength, chatting with everyone in turn. In particular, he seemed to get on well with Colonel Ramsay. They discussed the history of the tiny town and the marshes and it seemed they had mutual acquaintances in the district.

Pepper looked fabulous in a long skirt of autumnal colours topped with a high-necked white blouse. Her ear-rings were exquisite, long pendants of subdued colours to match her skirt, colours which flashed enticingly when she turned her head and the light caught them.

Annabel herself was wearing a black light-woollen sheath dress with long sleeves and high neck. She had a diamond bracelet on her right wrist and she wore matching ear-rings.

As she sat now wondering whether the evening had really been a success, she felt more lonely than ever. She wondered what Alex was doing this evening, if he had heard that she was giving a party and what would he think about it? She poured herself a small brandy and decided to go to bed as soon as she had finished it. Pepper's maid was coming back in the morning to clear away the remnants of the party and stash the dirty plates and glasses into the dish washer. I've grown idle Annabel thought, I'll have to do these chores for myself in the future. It'll be good for me. I've got to pull myself together and make a new life.

She was halfway through her drink when the doorbell rang. She glanced round quickly to see if there was anything left behind, like a handbag, keys, but she could see nothing and then the bell rang again. Puzzled, she got up and went to answer it.

Joe Linden stood outside proffering a bottle of brandy.

'A small contribution.'

'The guests have gone. The party's over.'

He grinned at her. 'This guest has only just

arrived. Is he going to be let in?'

'I was about to go to bed.' But she moved aside for him to enter.

'People die in bed,' he said, moving past her and placing the brandy bottle on a small table. 'Didn't you know that?'

He reached for a couple of glasses from a tray on which there were some clean ones and poured a measure of brandy into two of them, handing one to her. She moved with the glass back to her chair, indicating to him that he should sit in another chair by the window. Before sitting down with his drink, he stared out of the french windows which opened on to the balcony.

'Bloody dreary view. Why don't you sit on the side by the sea?'

'Because I prefer this one,' she replied stiffly.

He shrugged, turned the chair and straddled it, staring at her as he lifted his glass to her.

'Here's to party time.'

She put down her glass, picked up the one from which she had been drinking before his arrival and poured the contents into the one Joe Linden had given her.

He raised his eyebrows.

'Solitary drinking? Surely it doesn't have to be like this?'

'I'd hardly call a nightcap solitary drinking.'

He looked behind him into the room.

'Seems to me you've got chores to do before

124

you go to bed.'

'I'm lucky. A friend is lending me a member of her staff to come in tomorrow morning to clear up.'

Before he could say anything, she added quickly, 'I know what you're going to say and I'm not a poor little rich girl and the sooner I start to shoulder my own problems, the better it will be for me, but I'm not quite ready yet and I have very sympathetic understanding friends.'

He took an appreciative drink of brandy.

'Far be it from me to criticize such a well-organized person. Divorce is no big deal you know, it happens all the time.'

She smiled faintly.

'And you should know?'

'Yes, I should. I've been through it.'

Before she could answer the phone rang.

She got up and went across the room to answer it. It was David Seymour as she was afraid it would be.

'You haven't gone to bed then, Annabel?'

'No. I'm having a nightcap.'

She didn't speak his name. Somehow she didn't want to, with Joe Linden listening.

'It was a nice party, Annabel.'

'Yes, I thought so. Not exactly the social event of the year, but pleasant.'

'You sound a bit subdued. Are you all right?'

'Yes. Just a bit tired.'

'Well, I'll let you get to bed. I'll be running Ellie round tomorrow morning to clear up for you and I'll collect the empties and take them to the bottle bank for you.'

'It's very good of you.' Again something stopped her from speaking his name. 'But I can run them to the bottle bank in my car later.'

'No need. I'll do it for you. It's no trouble, it's on my way back.'

'Well, I'll run Ellie back when she's finished here.'

'You don't have to,' David said. 'She's not coming straight back here. She's going on to her sister's and her sister lives quite near you.'

'Oh. Well, thank you for ringing and thanks again for all your help.'

'Annabel,' he said sharply, 'are you sure you're all right?'

'Yes, of course.'

'Only you sound a bit . . .'

'A bit what?'

'Well, stilted somehow, but if you're sure you're OK.'

'Yes, I am, and thanks again for calling. I'll see you in the morning.'

'Annabel, you didn't get a visit from your ex after we'd all left, did you?'

She was surprised. 'Alex? No. Why would you think that?'

'No reason, except that we were told he was here in the hotel bar this evening.'

'Oh.'

She was momentarily at a loss, then she asked, 'Alone?'

126

'Yes.'

'So what happened?'

'Nothing. He had a couple of drinks and then left. I thought he might have heard about your party and decided to gate-crash it after we'd all left.'

She was surprised to hear that Alex had been in the Crown and alone. She wished that David would get off the line and that Joe Linden would go home so that she could be alone to think.

'Annabel, are you still there?'

'Yes. Thank you for calling. I'll see you in the morning.'

'Annabel, are you absolutely sure you're all right?'

'Yes. Why wouldn't I be?'

'I don't know. You sound a bit strange. Well, if you're sure, I'll say goodnight.'

'Goodnight,' she replied. 'I'll see you tomorrow and thanks again for all your help.'

She replaced the receiver and went back to sit down beside Joe Linden.

'It's not the end of the world, Annabel.'

'What isn't?'

'Divorce.'

'Tell me something,' she said, 'why did someone as obviously cynical as you ever get married in the first place.'

He gave a low chuckle.

'If I said it was the only way I could get my girl into bed?'

127

'I find that hard to believe.'

'You prefer to think I'm a sentimental fool who thinks it's for real every time?'

She affected a yawn.

'I'm too tired to know what I think. Does it matter anyway?'

He drained his glass and stood up.

'No, it doesn't matter a bloody damn, and I can take a hint.'

Annabel rose too. She moved back into the room, picked up the brandy bottle and proffered it to him. He brushed it aside.

'Keep it. Your late-night caller might come round to help you finish it.'

'What late-night caller?'

'The guy who just phoned you.'

'How do you know it was a man?'

'Oh, come on, sweetie. You never once spoke his name and you didn't tell him you had a male guest here.'

'I didn't have to. Who I have here is *my* business.'

His eyes roved over her assessingly.

'Well, you won't be alone for long, Annabel. In spite of taking this flat as a gesture of independence, you're not the type to travel alone.'

'I managed all right before I met my husband.'

'Ah, but then you hadn't known the joys of marriage.'

They were standing close together near the

door. She gave a nervous little laugh.

'You wouldn't be collecting material for your next book by any chance? Like the downfall of a clinging, helpless female?'

He grinned. 'You've obviously never read any of my books.'

'I don't know that I want to after speaking to Tracy Atkins tonight.'

He had put his arms on the wall either side of her so that she was imprisoned. She was dismayed to find herself responding to the sheer magnetism of this man and she was ashamed. It was a new feeling for her, nothing like the way she had felt with Alex. With Alex it had been a kind of extension of a schoolgirl crush into young love-play without urgency and passion. The way she felt with this man was quite different. It made her scared of her own desires. She knew that she desperately wanted to be held by him, have him make love to her. You're nothing but a tramp, Annabel Clifton, she told herelf, no better than Rosemary Wharton.

'Tracy Atkins,' he said, resuming the conversation after her last remark, 'is a silly little girl, playing at being a woman of the world. Her parents should be shot, allowing a kid like that to live in a flat alone.'

'Maybe she hasn't any parents.'

'Oh yes she has; decent, respectable people, running a decent, respectable boarding-house in Broadstairs.'

'You seem to know a lot about it.'

He grinned and Annabel thought it made him look absurdly young.

'Oh, I get around and I hear things, but why are we wasting precious time talking about stupid little Tracy Atkins?'

His arms slid down from the wall and encircled her waist. Before she could get her breath, he had fastened his lips on hers. She could taste the brandy on his mouth and the hardness of his body against her made her weak with longing, the kind of desperate longing she'd never felt before. She wanted this man, she wanted him to make love to her. With a sigh he eased himself away from her, but she clung to him, pressing her mouth to his again. He kissed her savagely whilst his hands strayed over her breasts, stroking, caressing, in contrast to the urgency of his mouth.

'Why, you're starved, my beauty,' he whispered. 'What kind of man was he, this slick estate agent?'

Without waiting for her reply, he took her by the hand and led her back into the room.

'I want to make love to you, Annabel, tonight, now.'

'I know. I want it too.'

'You're absolutely sure?'

She turned, her hand still in his, and led the way to the bedroom.

'Oh yes, I'm sure,' she said. 'Absolutely sure.'

CHAPTER FOURTEEN

Annabel had just emerged from the shower when the doorbell rang. She looked at the clock, ten o'clock. It must be the maid David was bringing round to clear up after the party. She was surprised to realize that she felt no guilt at facing David. In fact, she was basking in a wonderful sense of well-being, as if she was just starting out on a new adventure. Instead of making her feel ashamed, last night's loving with Joe Linden had given her a new confidence. She had no regrets. She answered the door to find Pepper standing outside with Ellie, the maid.

'Oh Pep. I'm so sorry, I'm not even dressed yet.'

'That's all right, kid. Do you feel up to making us some coffee whilst Ellie here starts on the clearance work?'

'Of course.'

Annabel stood aside for them to enter.

Ellie took a plastic apron from her large bag. 'You leave it to me Mrs Clifton. I'll soon have the place to rights for you.'

'Thanks Ellie. You're a gem.'

As she ushered Pepper into the kitchen Annabel said, 'I thought David was coming round with Ellie.'

'He was, but a traveller came in and collared him. Disappointed are you?'

Annabel laughed.

'No, of course not. It's lovely to see you, Pep.'

She busied herself with the coffee machine whilst Pepper seated herself on a kitchen stool, her long legs curled round the pedestal.

'You look like the cat that's nicked the cream, Annie. I think that party did you good.'

Annabel smiled a secret smile.

'Yes it did.'

Pepper eyed her intently. 'Has something happened, Annie? You look different.'

'How different?'

'Well, sort of smug-like; oh, I don't know how to put it. As if you've had good news or something.' Suddenly wary she asked, 'Alex hasn't been getting at you, has he?'

'No. I've heard nothing of Alex except that David rang me after the party last night and said that Alex was in your hotel whilst my party was in progress.'

'Yes, that's right.'

So it's not Alex, Pepper thought, but Annabel *is* different today. It's not David surely? Has she fallen for David? It would be wonderful if she *could* fall for David.

'So David rang you last night?'

'Yes,' admitted Annabel. 'I think it was just to tell me that Alex had been into your hotel.'

Pepper grinned.

'Or just another chance to talk to you. You know, don't you Annie, that David is more than halfway in love with you?'

'David? He can't be. He hardly knows me.'

'How long does it take to fall in love?'

Annabel was disconcerted.

'You can't be serious, Pep. David is so self-contained, a confirmed loner. I could never visualize David falling madly in love with anyone.'

'David was hurt once,' said Pepper, 'badly, and it's taken a long time to heal, but . . .'

'Oh no, Pep,' Annabel interrupted her. 'You've got it all wrong.'

She thought of the passion she had shared only a short while ago with Joe Linden and, for the first time, she experienced a stab of guilt. Had she somehow betrayed Pepper and David? That's stupid, she told herself, my private life is no concern of theirs, yet she did owe them honesty after all they had done for her, so she said now to Pepper, 'Just as I was about to go to bed last night Joe Linden arrived.'

'You didn't let him in, did you?'

Annabel took a cup of coffee to the maid who was tidying the sitting-room and when she came back she said, 'Yes. I let him in.'

'And?'

'I think I'm more than a little in love with him.'

Pepper untwisted her legs from the stool and sat bolt upright.

'Christ!' said Pepper. 'My poor innocent!'

She took a sip of her coffee before she went on, 'You do know nothing good will come of it, don't you?'

'I haven't really thought about it.'

'Annie, my sweetheart, you need a nursemaid. You're just an infant where men like Joe Linden are concerned. He's had three wives for Chrissake and God knows how many flings and mistresses.'

'So?'

'So I would have thought that, after Alex with his one small infidelity, Joe Linden would have looked like Satan to you.'

'Joe Linden doesn't owe me any loyalty: Alex did.'

'So what happens next?'

Annabel smiled dreamily.

'Who knows?'

'Did he tell you he loved you?'

'I can't remember.'

'Oh, honestly, Annie! What *have* you done?'

'Nothing, except grab myself some happiness.'

'With no future in it.'

'Maybe I don't want it to have any future.'

'So you're gonna sit here to be available to Joe Linden every time he feels randy.'

'It wasn't like that, Pep.'

'What was it like then? Did he ask you to marry him?'

'Of course not. He hardly knows me.'

134

Pepper uttered a curt laugh.

'I'd say he knows you pretty well—in the Biblical sense anyway.'

Annabel put her arms above her head in a sweeping gesture.

'I feel free, Pep. I know now that I was never completely satisfied when I was married to Alex. I was always sort of waiting for it to happen, for him to betray me, and he did, with that Wharton woman.'

'And now?'

Annabel shrugged. 'Who knows?'

'Did Joe Linden make you any promises of fidelity, and is there going to be a repeat performance of last night?'

'I wouldn't know.'

Pepper's usual flippancy seemed to have deserted her.

She was really worried about her friend.

'I think Jess was probably right when she said you'd be living in the evil belt between the sea and the canal.'

Annabel laughed. 'Oh Pep. Not you too. I didn't think you'd believe that nonsense.'

'I didn't. That is, until now.'

'It's not the end of the world, Pep.' Suddenly anxious she added, 'You won't tell David about Joe Linden, will you?'

Getting up from her chair Pepper said, 'No. Of course not. I wouldn't want to hurt him anyway.' She looked at her friend. 'Don't hurt him, Annie. I'm very fond of David and I'd hate to see him hurt again.'

Suddenly serious Annabel asked, 'Are *you* in love with him, Pep?'

Pepper gave a short laugh. 'Heavens, no. There's nothing like that between David and me, but we do go back a long way and we do care for each other.'

She picked up her handbag.

'I must be on my way, Annie. I've got to go to the bank and the supermarket. Ellie will make her own way when she's finished here.'

Annabel went with her friend to the door.

'Pep,' she said, 'I don't want to hurt anyone. I'm sorry if I've made you angry.'

'You haven't made me angry, just more than a little anxious.'

She bent over and planted a light kiss on Annabel's cheek.

'Keep smiling, honey. Things can only get better from now on. I'll be in touch. Ciao.'

CHAPTER FIFTEEN

Jessie looked up as Albert came into the kitchen.

'You've put your new suit on.'

He smiled. 'Yes. I thought it was time I gave it an airing. I've only worn it once or twice.'

'It's too good to wear for work, Albert.'

'Oh, I don't think so, Jess. Got to keep up

136

appearances you know. After all, Freeman & Son is the most prestigious firm in town. Wouldn't do for the owner to go about looking shabby.'

'I've never seen you looking shabby, Albert. You always look very smart to me.'

'You're biased, Jess.'

She peered at him anxiously. 'Have you nearly finished all that extra paperwork you were doing at the store?'

'Almost.' Albert sighed. He realized that he would have to stop the after-closing-time sessions with Laura now that feelings were so tense between them.

'Good.'

Jessie winced and put a hand to her chest.

'Are you all right, Jess?'

She smiled feebly. 'Yes. Just that sharp stabbing pain occasionally. Indigestion I think. Toast must have gone down the wrong way.'

'As I've said before, Jess, why don't you call and see Doc Willard?'

'I don't want to take up his precious time with a trivial pain.'

'But you've had it for some time now.'

Jessie moved over and planted a kiss on his cheek.

'Don't fuss, Albert. If it gets any worse I promise I'll go to see him.' She sniffed. 'You smell very nice this morning.'

'It's that aftershave I got at Inmans. They were out of my usual one.'

'It's almost nice enough for me to wear.' She gave a little shiver. 'Oh, I shall be so glad when this winter's over. It seems to be dragging on and on.'

Albert picked up his briefcase and moved to the door.

'What are you doing today then, Jess?'

'I'm having coffee this morning with Dora Hunter-Bell to discuss our next sale of work, but I'll be back at lunchtime if you want to come home for a sandwich.'

'No,' said Albert. 'I've got Transom's traveller coming in this morning. We'll probably go along about twelve to the Red Lion for a glass of wine and a sandwich and that'll keep me going until this evening.'

Jessie regarded him anxiously.

'You're not working late again tonight, Albert, are you?'

'No love. Be home at the usual time.' He bent and kissed her on the cheek. 'Bye now. Take care. Don't do too much and bring that pain on. See you usual time this evening.'

When he'd gone Jessie opened the kitchen window just a fraction. For some reason the perfume of Albert's aftershave bothered her. It was far too, she searched for the right word, exotic, that was it, too exotic, not like Albert's usual scent which was just pleasant and not at all intrusive.

The maid, Maisie Webb, arrived and Jessie forgot about Albert's new aftershave. As

Maisie started to clear the breakfast-table she said, 'I passed Mr Freeman on 'is way to the car. A real smart man is Mr Freeman, always looks the part, don't he?'

'What part?'

'Well, you know, the successful businessman.'

'Well, he *is* a successful businessman,' said Jessie curtly.

Oh Gawd, thought Maisie, in one of 'er moods today, is she?

'I'm going out at eleven,' said Jessie, 'to meet Mrs Hunter-Bell.'

'Yes, well,' said Maisie stiffly, she wasn't prepared to be snubbed again. 'It's bedrooms day today, so I'll get 'em done soon, just as soon as I've done down 'ere. Then, this afternoon, I'll strip orf them loose covers and give 'em a good shakin' in the garden if it stays fine.'

At half past ten Jessie went upstairs to change into her thick tweed suit. It was, she thought, rather cold today, so instead of a blouse she put on a light woollen sweater under her jacket. Dora Hunter-Bell usually wore a hat during the winter months, so Jessie donned a tam-o-shanter-type hat of the same maroon shade as her shirt with a cairngorm brooch pinned on the front. She peered at herself in the mirror. The hat hid the grey in her hair, but did it look just a trifle skittish? She thought of Albert, going off this morning in his

139

smart suit. Albert has aged better than I have, she thought despairingly. Albert, just lately, has seemed extraordinarily ebullient, whereas I, she decided forlornly, seem to have grown old and drab suddenly. Annabel's behaviour hasn't helped, she excused herself, the worry of Annabel's marital problems has been a burden I've had to shoulder alone. Albert hasn't really been any help, and this tiresome indigestion has been dragging me down.

The pain stabbed now and she sat down on the bed, waiting for it to pass. I wonder why Albert and I haven't been blessed with children? She had always been too shy to discuss the matter with Albert and he had never voiced any desire for a family. The pain passed and she got up again, trying to force herself into a lighter mood. I'm a lucky woman really. I have a lovely home, a good Christian husband, no money worries. Soon I shall suggest that Albert retires and puts a manager or manageress into the store, then we can spend more time together, play bowls maybe, give more time to the bridge club, organize more outings for the church and the WI. More cheerful now, she sallied forth to meet Dora Hunter-Bell.

Jess and Dora met for coffee in an old-established coffee shop in the centre of the small town. Dora was already seated when Jessie arrived. On her way over to Dora's table Jessie nodded and smiled at the few local traders and professional men who took their coffee each morning at the Malt House. It was like a club, she thought, select and in no way like other small restaurants in the town which were patronized by holidaymakers and foreign students.

'You look pale, Jessie,' said Dora, as Jessie seated herself beside her friend. 'Are you all right?'

'Yes. I'm fine,' Jessie said, unbuttoning her jacket. She attempted flippancy. 'All set to launch the sale of work.' She turned as the waitress approached. 'Coffee with cream please, Marie.'

'Very good, Mrs Freeman.'

'How's Albert?' asked Dora Hunter-Bell.

'Fine. Very busy at the store. In fact, he's had to work into the evenings lately, which is most unusual, but he says there's a lot of paperwork to catch up on.'

'Does he work there alone?'

Jessie looked surprised.

'Oh yes. No one but Albert ever touches the books.'

Dora was silent a moment, then she said abruptly, 'What about that young woman who lives with her widowed mother in Wilbur Parade, Laura Collins I think her name is? She's worked in Albert's store ever since she left school I think.'

Again Jessie was surprised. Albert had never mentioned Laura Collins, but then Albert

141

seldom discussed the staff with her.

'What about Laura Collins?' she asked her friend.

Dora Hunter-Bell toyed with her coffee spoon.

'Well, I heard that she stays late at the store sometimes and that she's been seen leaving with Albert in his car.'

Jessie was shocked and the pain in her upper chest flared violently. She put a hand up in a quick gesture of repudiation.

'What's the matter, Jessie? Are you in pain?'

'No. Yes, well, just a little.' Jessie mustered a weak, apologetic smile. 'I've been having little pains lately in the upper chest. I think it's indigestion. Albert wants me to see Doctor Willard. Laura Collins you said, Dora? She's a sort of manageress, I think. I did hear once that she had a son at boarding-school so I suppose there must be a husband somewhere. She was in Albert's car, you say? There must be some mistake. Albert would have mentioned it to me.'

'Yes, of course,' said Dora soothingly. She was a little alarmed at the pallor of Jessie's face and wished now that she hadn't broached the subject, but Jessie was not prepared to relinquish it.

'Who told you the woman was in Albert's car?'

Dora smiled thinly. 'Well, you know what gossips these cleaning women are, but the woman, Janey Evans, who cleans for me told me she was in her friend's flat opposite your store recently and they saw Albert helping the Collins girl into his car a couple of hours after the store had officially closed.'

Jessie was shocked to the core. Why hadn't Albert mentioned it? Of course, there was nothing in it, just Albert's kindness in doing a favour for one of his employees, but then, why hadn't he told her about it? He always told her everything that happened in the store. Her mind worked furiously. Albert and Laura Collins! Oh no. Albert was too dignified to make friends with an employee, and a female one at that. It must be a pack of wicked lies.

'Lies,' she said now to Dora. 'Albert doesn't consort with his employees after business hours.'

'Probably. You know what gossips these women are, but it's a strange thing for them to invent, don't you think?' Dora shrugged.

Jessie was silent. The shock of Dora's disclosures had made her feel sick.

'Jessie,' Dora said, alarmed now at her friend's silence and pallor. 'Take no notice, Jessie. It's just jealous malicious gossip, it must be. How's your sister making out? I hear she's taken one of the flats in Romney Place where Colonel Ramsay lives.'

Jessie looked blank. Her mind was still on Albert and Laura Collins.

'Quite expensive those flats,' Dora went on,

'considering they're in the so-called evil belt. Jessie dear, are you sure you're all right?'

Jessie stared at her friend and Dora was alarmed at the look in Jessie's eyes—mingled bewilderment and hurt.

'Jessie!'

Jessie tried to pull herself together.

'Yes Dora, I'm fine, but do you mind if I don't stay now to discuss the sale of work? You see, I've just remembered I've got a man coming to see about building Albert a shed behind our garage.'

Dora Hunter-Bell was quite sure that this was a lie. Jessie Freeman was far too well organized to mix up her appointments. Wasn't she one of the most reliable of the welfare workers, always in control of her commitments? Jessie Freeman wouldn't have come out to coffee if she'd had to see a man about a shed. No. It must have been the revelations about Laura Collins and Albert which had upset her.

Jessie pushed her coffee cup away.

'The coffee tastes sour this morning. Last night's warmed up, I think. If you'll excuse me, Dora, I *must* go. I'll ring you when I've sorted myself out.' She attempted a weak smile. 'If you pay for the coffee this morning, I'll pay next time.'

She was too confused to hear her friend's reply. Rising to her feet and clutching her handbag, she made her way erratically between the tables and out into the street, ignoring friendly smiles from the other patrons. Albert and Laura Collins! No. It was a lie. It must be. She didn't know how she got home, but somehow, much later it seemed, she was lying on the sofa with Maisie Webb fluttering over her.

'Don't you move now, Mrs Freeman, I'm gonna call the doctor.'

Gasping for breath, Jessie thought she was dying. She tried to put out a hand to keep Maisie beside her, but she hadn't enough strength to raise her arm. From a distance she heard the maid's voice talking on the phone. After what seemed an eternity, the woman came back and knelt down beside her.

'Doc's on 'is way, dear. I just caught 'im between calls. I rung Mr Freeman too and he's on 'is way home.'

She took Jessie's hands in her own and rubbed them gently.

'Are you cold, love?'

Jessie felt too ill to speak, but her brain was spinning with dreadful, confusing thoughts. Albert and a woman called Laura Collins! Annabel, divorce, evil, Annabel living between the sea and the canal. Help Mumma, help. It's not true, is it? Much later it seemed a man's voice cut into her dreadful fantasies.

'You're going to be all right, Jess dearest. Rest now, Jess dearest, rest.'

Albert, but Albert never calls me 'dearest'.

Something is wrong. Help me, Mumma. Help me.

CHAPTER SIXTEEN

Annabel smiled weakly.

'I feel like a traitor going off to enjoy myself whilst my sister is in hospital.'

'Nonsense. You can't help her by staying here. You've been told that her condition is satisfactory, that all she needs now is rest and, after all, her husband is within easy call.'

'Even so . . .'

He put an arm around her and drew her to him.

'Last night you said a day in London was your idea of heaven, a mosey round the West End dress shops, a lunch together somewhere glamorous and then a drive back here to your place or mine.' He laughed wickedly. 'Whichever bed we reach first.'

He draped her jacket over her shoulders as she locked the door of her flat. Annabel put her hand on Joe Linden's arm.

'Right. Let's away then before my conscience pulls me back.'

As she snuggled into the seat of his BMW she thought briefly of Pepper and David. Although she had phoned Pepper each day, she hadn't seen her or David since she had fallen in love with Joe Linden. Although Pepper had said nothing, Annabel sensed that she didn't approve of Joe. As for David, he had dropped into the background of her life where he had been before her separation from Alex.

Joe glanced down at her as she snuggled into the collar of her jacket.

'Settled everything with your ex?'

She was silent a moment, then she sat up straight.

'Yes. It was easier than I thought. He's selling the Copmarsh house and moving to London. He offered me half the proceeds of the sale and a generous allowance, but I refused all his offers. It would be wrong of me to accept, particularly as I left *him*. My parents saw to it that I was left with sufficient means to look after myself. Do you know, I thought it would upset me to see Alex again, but when I did, I realized that I'd never really loved him. It was like a schoolgirl crush—handsome, amusing playboy, silly, innocent girl who believed in loving by the story-book rules. He must have found me such a bore. As for me, he was the prince in the panto and when he let me down I reacted like a lovesick child. I'm not a child now, am I Joe? I've grown up, thanks to you.'

He grinned down at her.

'I hope you have. No one should expect a monopoly of another person's life. That's why marriage is such an out-dated institution.'

'Yet you've been married.'

He grimaced.

'Only because I'm a silly sod who doesn't heed his own doctrine.'

His callous words grated on her, but she told herself not to be so sensitive. It was Joe's pose to pretend to be cynical. Deep down he was really very tender.

'Were you ever in love with your wives?'

His mouth hardened. 'No inquest, honey. Subject boring.'

She sank back in her seat.

'Sorry. I didn't mean to be tedious.'

He took his left hand from the wheel and ran it down her leg.

'With legs like yours you could never be tedious, my sweet.'

He put his hand back on the steering wheel.

'Better keep my mind on the road. I'm not conditioned to driving with one hand.'

Annabel luxuriated into gentle happiness as the car raced towards London. She told herself she was well and truly happy for the first time in her life. She thought briefly of Jessie and Albert. Their marriage had always seemed such a humdrum affair, yet Albert had appeared to be totally stricken when Jess had collapsed, but Jess was going to be all right so Annabel thrust her sister out of her mind and concentrated on her own happiness that had come to her just when she thought her heart was broken. There was nothing now to stop her divorce proceeding smoothly. When it was finalized there would be just Joe and herself, two mature people who had found real happiness at last.

So, the prestigious car sped on towards London and Annabel dreamed her rosy dreams.

*   *   *

Pale sunshine lightened the window of the small private ward at St Martin's Nursing Home. The pretty cretonne curtains lifted slightly in the faint breeze. Albert remembered the substantial order given to his store for the cretonne—one of his more expensive lines. Everything at St Martin's Nursing Home was of the highest quality from the highly skilled respectful staff down to the cleaners who ensured the clinical cleanliness of the nursing home with unobtrusive efficiency. Yes, Albert decided, Jess couldn't have been in a more prestigious hospital.

'It's almost spring now, Jessie,' he said. 'Already the sun is getting stronger.'

Jessie smiled weakly. 'I'm keeping you away from the store.'

Albert bent over the bed and planted a light kiss on his wife's forehead.

'You're more important than the store, Jess, my love.'

'Am I, Albert? Really?'

149

'Of course you are, Jess. You must know that.' She turned her face into the pillow and her voice was muffled. 'Once I thought I knew. Now I'm not sure.'

'Jessie! You're my wife. I couldn't go on living without *you*.'

Her voice was faint and he strained to hear.

'"Don't sit under the apple tree with anyone else but me". You remember, Albert, we used to sing that old song when I played the piano in my parents' drawing-room when we were courting?'

'Yes. I remember Jess, and we'll play it again when you come home. It's time we used our piano instead of watching television all the time.'

Jessie gave a feeble giggle.

'What will Maisie think?'

'Ah, Maisie,' he said. 'Yes, I'm glad she's come to live in. We should have done that from the start, then maybe you wouldn't have taken ill.'

'It wasn't housework that made me sick,' Jessie said. 'It was what Dora Hunter-Bell said about you and that .. that saleswoman in your store.'

Albert was temporarily at a loss. Jessie's words—'that saleswoman in your store' seemed to reduce his very dear Laura into someone cheap and insignificant. He felt like a Judas when he said now, 'There *was* no important saleswoman in my store, Jess. She was just a

150

trusted employee helping me sort out some staffing problems and discrepancies.'

Forgive me, Lord, he prayed silently. I've sinned. I've betrayed two good women.

'All that matters, Jess,' he continued aloud, 'is that you get better quickly so that we can get on with our lives.'

Jessie lifted a hand and Albert gently enclosed it in his.

'I don't want to be an invalid, Albert.'

'You won't be, Jess, but you *will* have to take things more quietly; let Dora Hunter-Bell take more of the strain on the good-works front.'

Jessie sighed. 'Oh she will. She's very efficient is Dora and I know she feels guilty for telling me about that . . . that woman . . .' Her voice trailed off, her eyes clouded.

Albert bent over her. 'Forget it, Jess. I've told you it's not important, just malicious gossip.'

'Yes, I suppose so.' A little gleam lit her eyes. 'I think Dora *must* feel guilty because she sent all those very expensive flowers.' She turned her head towards the big bowls of flowers on the window sill of the small private room.

'Yes,' said Albert, 'and Annabel has sent lovely flowers too. *And* she's ringing all the time to check your progress, as have many people from the church. You're a very much-loved woman, Jess.'

Jessie smiled again, more strongly this time.

'As long as *you* love me, Albert, I don't care

151

about the others. I'll even try to stop worrying about Annabel and her new lifestyle if God will let me get better.'

'I'm sure He will,' said Albert soothingly. 'God will look after His faithful followers.'

Please God, he prayed silently, let Jessie get better and I promise I'll never sin again. Ah, Laura my lovely, I'm sure you'll understand. You came into my life too late.

It was two days later when Laura confronted Albert in his office at the store. She hovered in the doorway, a half smile on her lips.

'Have you got a minute?'

He noticed that she didn't call him 'Mr Freeman' as she had always done in the past.

'Of course, Laura. Come in.'

He gestured towards a chair, but she remained standing.

'How's Mrs Freeman?'

'Making good steady progress. We're to have her home at the end of the week.'

'Oh, I'm so glad. You said "we"?'

'Yes. Our daily is living in now.'

'I see.'

She twisted her hands together and he thought how elegant they were, in keeping with the rest of her, fresh, sweet and elegant. She had breathed springtime into his life so briefly, now she was lost to him for ever.

'Laura . . .' He moved towards her, but she stepped back a pace.

'Mr Freeman.' Her voice dropped a tone.

'Albert . . .'

'Yes Laura?'

'I don't know quite how to say this, but I think it would be better for all concerned if I left Freeman's.'

Albert was shocked.

'Left?' he repeated stupidly. 'After all these years?'

She looked at him squarely. 'I love you Albert, but I can't go on seeing you and knowing . . .' Her voice faltered, then she rallied and her voice was firm again. 'Ivor Meadows, head of men's wear at Jason's of Canterbury has offered me a job as head of ladies' separates.'

Albert felt as if he'd been punched in the stomach.

'Jason's?' he repeated stupidly. 'He wants you to leave Freeman's?'

'Yes. I met him at bingo. I was introduced to him by one of my mother's friends.' Almost apologetic now she added, 'I was feeling terribly down when your wife collapsed and I let myself be talked into going to one of the bingo sessions at St Mark's hall. That's where I met Mr Meadows. He was with his niece. He's a widower you see.'

'Jason's?' Albert said, shaking his head in bewilderment. 'But you'd spend so much time travelling.'

'No. Mr Meadows has a car. He'd ferry me back and forth.'

Laura, spending time each day with an eligible man in a car! Albert felt again as if he'd been hit in the stomach.

'I can't think of Freeman's without you, Laura.'

She sighed. 'No. I can't either. It's been such a huge part of my life for so long but, as my mother says'—a faint smile lit her eyes—' "there's an end to everything and everything has an end".' More firmly now she continued, 'I know it's not my place to tell you what to do with your staff, but Brenda Hill in curtains is a very competent and loyal employee and I'm sure she could take over from me without any trouble.'

Albert thought of Brenda Hill, spinster, a plain, drab woman who seldom smiled, but he knew she was super efficient and very honest. Even so, after Laura, *his* Laura . . .

'Don't you see, Albert,' Laura continued gently, 'we never stood a chance, you and I. We met too late and we can't take our happiness if it's going to destroy someone else; we'd never be able to live with it.'

Albert wanted to sit down and cry, which he hadn't done since he was a very young schoolboy, but he knew Laura was right. It had been a lovely, impossible dream and now it was over. Ivor Meadows, Jason's of Canterbury!

'Right, Laura,' he said heavily. 'Let me know when you want to go and I'll make the necessary arrangements, references and so

154

forth.' The ghost of a smile played over his mouth. 'I guess the staff will want to make a presentation to you after all your years with the store.'

'Oh, I wouldn't want that,' she said desperately. 'I don't think I could bear it.'

'We've both got to bear it, Laura,' he said quietly. 'We must smile and try to hide our heartbreak.'

I'm talking like a corny movie he thought but, oddly enough, I mean it. There's no other way to say it. Love *is* corny.

'Right,' she said, turning away so that he wouldn't see the tears starting in her eyes. 'Then I won't waste any more of your time Albert .. Mr Freeman. I'll make sure everything is in apple-pie order in my department before I leave.'

'I know you will, Laura,' he said heavily. 'I know you will. Goodbye.'

CHAPTER SEVENTEEN

Annabel was humming happily to herself as she went down the stairs and out to the garage to get her car. As she had let herself out of her flat, Tracy Atkins had appeared at the top of the staircase but, on seeing Annabel, had turned abruptly and gone back inside her flat.

Annabel grinned to herself. Obviously the

155

girl knew that Joe Linden was lost to her and she couldn't face the opposition. Well, I know what it feels like, Annabel thought smugly, but I'm over that now. I've got Joe to look after me from now on. That's why I shall be able to face this last meeting with Alex with so little pain.

She had agreed to meet Alex for lunch at a small pub on the marshes. He had said he wanted to consult her on the division of certain small items in the house before it was finally vacated.

When she had asked Joe's advice he'd simply shrugged and said, 'Why not? We're all civilized people. Sleep with the guy one last time if that's what you both want. Might be a good idea to get him out of your system.'

Annabel had been shocked, but she was gradually getting used to Joe's flippancy now. She told herself it was a pose with him, that he was trotting out the kind of dialogue he used in his books which, Pepper told her, were full of cynical hard-bitten characters. Like a small boy playing out cowboy fantasies, Annabel thought indulgently. At heart Joe is just a softie. She smiled to herself as she drove to her rendezvous with Alex. Joe was away for three days in Wiltshire to do, he said, some research for another book. When she had offered to go with him he'd firmly turned down her offer. 'I want to work, baby, not screw myself into oblivion.' Some of Joe's speech offended her but, she told herself, she'd lived a sheltered life

156

long enough. There was another world outside Copmarsh and she would, sooner or later, have to face it, but Joe would be there beside her.

She thought suddenly of Pepper and David. She knew they didn't approve of her relationship with Joe Linden and this saddened her somewhat, as they had been such a source of strength when she had finally decided to walk away from her marriage. Her own kin Jessie and Albert, had given her no support, just disapproval, of her decision to file for divorce, so Pepper and David had taken the place of family.

As she drove across the marshes she made up her mind to call at the Crown on her way home to have a chat with Pepper if she was in. She wanted so much for Pepper and David to share in her new happiness and, in time, maybe they would get to like Joe and they could, all four, have a good social life together. So Annabel dreamed as she drove.

Her heart gave a little lurch as Alex came to greet her at the Fisherman's Hut. He looked even more handsome than usual, she thought, in a light cashmere sweater and pale-grey trousers, a welcoming smile on his mouth, a flash of pleasure in his eyes. As she moved forward to greet him she thought of Joe—lean, sallow, the permanent demoniac gleam in his eyes and she realized that Alex had never moved her to such heights and depths as Joe Linden could, just by looking at her.

'You look wonderful, Annabel.'

'So do you, Alex.'

He took her arm and led her in to the bar.

'Let's have a drink whilst we order. Is it still martini?'

'Yes please.'

'Good to see some things don't change.' He smiled faintly.

Annabel didn't want to get involved in personalities. Briskly she asked, 'Do you have a list of the items you wanted to discuss, Alex?'

He gave a rueful grin. 'In other words, don't digress, as my sainted papa used to say when I was on the carpet.'

She was saved the necessity of a reply because Alex had to order the drinks and ask for a menu. When this had been done he turned to her.

'How are you liking your flat?'

'It's lovely. It has everything I need.'

'And you're not worried by the old superstition?'

'No.'

She thought suddenly of Joe and that first night they had together when he had suggested that she moved her seat to look out on the side with the sea view, instead of the canal.

'No,' she said again. 'It's just an old wives' tale. Life is what you make it.'

'That's a trite remark, quite unlike you, Annie. It smacks of Jessie methinks. By the way, how is she? I was sorry to hear of her

158

collapse.'

'She's got angina,' replied Annabel, 'but Albert says her condition is satisfactory. She'll just have to take life more quietly in future.'

Alex grinned at her over his whisky glass.

'I don't think Jessie ever led a *noisy* life.'

'No, but she did do a lot of charity work under the auspices of Dora Hunter-Bell.'

Alex pulled a face. 'That sanctimonious old trout.'

Annabel giggled. 'Yes she is, isn't she? She's never approved of *me*, I'm afraid.'

'Oh, Annie,' Alex said, suddenly serious. 'Does it really have to end? We had such a lot of fun together. Couldn't we just try . . .?'

Quickly she interrupted him.

'Alex, you promised, no heavy stuff, just a civilized discussion about property.'

'I'm still madly in love with you.'

'You'll get over it. I'm sure there are plenty of girls out there only too willing to compensate you. What about Rosemary Wharton?'

'She's going away, leaving Copmarsh.'

'With you?'

'No. Like the rotter I am, I ditched her. She bitched up my happiness, Annabel. She made me lose *you*. I hate her for it.'

Annabel took a good sip of her drink before she replied quietly, 'I seem to remember you bitched it up yourself, Alex. No one forced you to sleep with Rosemary Wharton. It's not very

159

gallant to blame her now. You're like the little boy who hogged too much candy, made himself sick and then blamed the candy.'

He was saved a reply by the arrival of a young girl in a black skirt and white blouse ushering them to a small table in the bar. As they sat down Alex said, 'Annabel, if you're ever short of money, you've got to promise to tell me.'

'I shan't be.' She smiled faintly. 'I'm what they call a good catch.'

He looked startled. 'Will you marry again?'

'Oh yes, I think so. In fact, I'm sure I will.'

'You've got someone?' His eyes grew bleak.

She was silent a moment, toying with the cheese sandwich which had been put before her, then she nodded.

'Anyone I know?'

'No. At least, you may know *of* him, but I don't think he mixes socially around here.'

The old petulant look that Annabel had come to know so well came over her ex-husband's face. Like a kid unable to get his own way, she thought.

'Listen, Alex,' she said. 'Let's not pry into each other's lives. I shall always wish you well and I hope we can be friends. When you're settled in London, let me have your address and phone number.' She smiled faintly and he wanted desperately to kiss her. 'We can send each other birthday cards.'

'Oh Annie . . .'

160

'No, Alex.' She looked away from the pleading in his eyes. 'The list, Alex.'

Finally he shrugged and took out his wallet from which he extracted a piece of paper which he handed to her.

'The furniture is being sold, but these are small things, pictures and the like.'

Annabel scanned the list. She put her finger on an item.

'That picture of the Virgin Mary and child.'

He gave a weak grin. 'Ghastly thing! I almost threw it out.'

'Oh, don't do that, Alex. Jess loves it. It belonged to our mother and Jess never forgave her for giving it to *me*. I offered to let Jess have it, but she went all huffy and refused it, but I think she will accept it now that things are different.'

'Too bloody different,' he said moodily. 'Oh, Annie, what a fool I've been.'

She put up a hand. 'No personalities, Alex, please. Let's play it cool and stay friends.'

He was sulkily silent for a while, toying with his food, then he said, 'This feller you're in love with, Annie, who is he?'

She wasn't sure she wanted to tell him, but the whole world would know soon.

'The writer, Joe Linden.'

'What?'

He pushed his plate away with a muffled oath.

'You must be mad, Annabel. The bloke's a

bloody disaster. He's had lots of wives, he's a well-known womanizer.'

'He's the victim of evil gossip,' said Annabel quietly. 'You don't know him, Alex. *I* do.'

'You didn't waste much time, did you?' he said bitterly. 'Were you seeing him before you and I broke up?'

'Certainly not. I met him when I moved into Romney Place. He has a flat there.'

'Oh Annie,' he said earnestly. 'You're such an innocent. Why have I been such a fool?'

By the time she reached the Crown Annabel was almost in tears. She hadn't anticipated her meeting with Alex upsetting her so much, but it was his condemnation of Joe that had been the final straw.

David Seymour came to greet her as she got out of her car in the hotel forecourt.

'Annabel! What a delightful surprise.'

Striving for self-control she said, 'Pepper?'

'Out I'm afraid. Will I do?' He took her by the arm. 'You look as if you need a drink.'

She shook her head as she allowed him to lead her into the hotel. Although it was an unseasonably mild day, she was shivering.

'I don't want a drink, thank you David.'

'Coffee then?'

His firm grip on her arm was reassuring. As they entered the hotel she struggled to regain control.

'Coffee would be lovely, David. Thank you.'

When he had seated her in his office and

ordered the coffee he asked, 'What's wrong, Annabel?'

'I've just had a meeting with Alex to decide what to . . .' She stopped, her lips trembling.

'Don't upset yourself, Annabel,' he said gently. 'I guess you'd rather wait until you talk to Pep.'

Annabel turned away from the compassion in his eyes. She gave a brittle laugh.

'I've just realized,' she said, 'that, after all, we didn't decide what to do with the items we arranged to discuss, except one dreary old picture of the Virgin Mary which I want to give to Jessie. Oh David, I seem to have made such a mess of things.'

'No you haven't, Annabel. Divorce is always traumatic. It takes an age to get life into proper perspective again.'

She threw him a tremulous smile.

'Of course, you've been through it, haven't you, and you seem to have survived.'

Before he could reply a waitress came in with a tray of coffee. When she had gone David said, 'Yes, I've survived, Annabel, but there is still a great void in my life.'

The look in his eyes strangely disturbed her. She told herself she shouldn't have come here. David and Pepper obviously didn't approve of the way she was handling the end of her marriage. As she drank her coffee she forced herself to talk to David about impersonal things—the other tenants in her block of flats, the superstition about the evil belt and when, at three o'clock, Pepper hadn't returned, she pleaded chores to do and left, thanking David for his time and the coffee.

Oh Annabel, he mourned silently as he saw her drive away, if only ... Joe Linden of all people, what a bloody disaster!

David Seymour went back to his duties in the hotel with a heavy heart.

CHAPTER EIGHTEEN

Albert Freeman had always been one of the most energetic members of the Chamber of Commerce, but lately he had been apathetic where before he had been a most enthusiastic contributor to the various activities and projects of the Chamber. Friends put it down to the shock he had received when his wife had so suddenly been taken ill and was having to cut down drastically on her own social life and her charities. At the store Albert was noticeably quiet and, at times, even absent-minded. Staff, too, attributed this to the sudden illness of Mrs Freeman. They didn't know that every time he entered the store his eyes swivelled to the desk where his beloved Laura had sat for so many years. Once, driving in extra early to the store, he had passed the car driven by Ivor Meadows. He had caught a glimpse of Laura in the front

164

passenger seat. After that he made sure he was not on that road at that time of the morning.

Albert thought he knew now the true meaning of the words 'a broken heart'. The staff presentation to Laura when she left had been sheer mental torture. He had himself organized Laura's parting present. Although he had pretended to seek the advice of Brenda Hill, the woman who was to take Laura's position in the store, Albert had definite ideas about Laura's present.

'Miss Collins is a dainty lady,' he'd told Brenda, 'and I think a single strand gold bracelet would be very fitting. I understand that real gold will cost a lot, but if members of staff will each make a modest contribution, I will personally make up the difference and, with your approval, of course, I will ask Mr Bidmead, the jeweller in South Street, to find us something suitable. I know him well and I'm sure he will give us good value for money. I'd like you to help me choose it, of course. Do you think that would be satisfactory to the rest of the staff?'

'Oh I'm sure it will be, Mr Freeman,' the woman had gushed. 'It's very generous of you, sir.'

'Not at all Miss Hall. Miss Collins has been a loyal and faithful member of Freeman's for many years and it's only fitting that she should have something nice to remind her of us.'

A thin gold bracelet is the nearest thing I can

get to a ring, my darling, he told Laura silently. He congratulated himself that he had got through Laura's presentation ceremony with great self-control. Only his dear Laura, pale but composed, had known what it was costing him. He could find no fault with Brenda Hill as Laura's replacement in the store. The woman was quietly efficient and popular with the rest of the staff. He discovered that she was forty years old and had been engaged for many years to the nephew of the local undertaker with no imminent prospect of marriage. So Albert hid his broken heart and life went on as usual at the store, with Brenda Hill taking Laura's place with efficiency.

At home, Albert was extra kind to Jessie, waiting on her hand and foot. As for Jessie, she grew tired quickly and was surprisingly apathetic towards her former charity work and church duties. The only strong feelings she expressed were directed towards her sister. By now it was common knowledge in the small town that Joe Linden and Annabel Clifton were lovers.

'If only Mumma were still alive,' Jessie fumed. '*She* wouldn't have allowed Annabel to make a fool of herself over a disgusting lecher like that writer. Just an animal he is by all accounts.'

'But Jess dear,' Albert had expostulated, 'if Annabel is determined to marry the man, I doubt if anything your dear mama could have said would stop her.'

'I blame that flighty Pepper Finlay,' Jessie said. 'She's a bad influence on Annabel. She must know that Annabel will never achieve happiness with a man like Joe Linden.'

Pepper *did* know and she was worried. She confided her fears to David Seymour. David admitted that he, too, was concerned.

'She's such a lovely unawakened girl,' he said. 'It was bad enough when she wasted herself on a selfish young oaf like Alex Clifton, but this Linden is way out of Clifton's league. The man is a disaster.'

And you'd give anything to have Annabel feel about you the way she feels about Linden, Pepper thought.

'Well, there's nothing we can do about it,' 'she said, 'except to be here for her when the crunch comes.'

Annabel was longing for the time when she and Joe could live together openly, but Joe said there was no hurry for that. They were both in the midst of divorce proceedings, they were living in the same building and, for him, that was a very satisfactory arrangement. They seldom went out together, except for the occasional dinner at one of the small hostelries on the marshes, and so life went on until the small town of Copmarsh was breathing the fragrant green freshness of spring.

Annabel's heart was light. She told herself that she had never been so happy. Joe was disinclined to discuss the future and where they would live after their respective divorces, but she was content to leave this matter in the air for the time being. It was a small thing compared with the love that had come into her life. Joe was a skilled and considerate lover, extraordinarily tender at times, and life with him was showing her just how inadequate Alex had been.

When Joe was busy writing Annabel visited friends, went into Canterbury shopping with Pepper and called regularly on Jessie to see if there was anything she could do for her sister. She put up with Jessie's lectures and disapproval of Joe, telling herself that when Jess was really better and she, Annabel, was married to Joe, then would be the time to try to establish a basis for a family relationship, although she knew in her heart that Joe would have little time for pious Albert. Still, she was too happy now to worry about such things.

The only little niggle in her newfound happiness was David Seymour. She had the feeling that he was deliberately avoiding her. Since the advent of Joe into her life David had made no contact with her. When he had first moved into the flat David had been in regular touch, offering assistance and advice. When she mentioned this to Pepper, Pepper said, 'Well, you've got Joe now to do all your little chores. I don't think he'd take kindly to David poking his nose in.'

'Oh, Joe's not possessive,' Annabel said. 'Neither is he much good at the little chores as you call them, not like David is.'

'Well, you can't have everything, sweetie,' Pepper had replied. 'You can't go to bed with Joe and expect David to come in and make the bed for you.'

Annabel laughed. 'Oh Pep, don't be so daft. As if I would!'

'David cares a lot for you,' Pepper told her, 'and it must hurt to see you so much in love with another man.'

After that conversation Annabel seldom mentioned David to Pepper. She saw very little of the other tenants of the flats. In fact, she wondered if Tracy Atkins had gone away, as there were no sounds from her flat, neither did they meet, as they used to, on the way to and from the garages. When she mentioned this to Joe he just shrugged and said, 'Oh, she's still around. She never mixed much with the other residents; they're too old for her I suppose.'

'Including me,' Annabel said lightly, but Joe didn't answer. He seemed disinclined to talk about the girl and showed little interest in the other tenants, so, wisely Annabel let the subject drop. She was learning fast how to cope with his moods. She told herself that writers, like actors, paid little attention to mundane matters. Joe loved her and that was enough.

At the beginning of May he announced that he was off to Glasgow for two weeks to do some research. She pleaded with him to allow her to accompany him.

'I won't get in your way, darling. I'll even stay cooped up in the hotel room if you wish, or go sight-seeing by myself on one of those organized tours. I promise I won't interfere with your work but'—she smiled at him seductively—'I'll be there in your bed at night.'

'That's the last thing I want when I'm working,' said Joe abruptly, 'bed.' He kissed her, then he added, 'You have to understand, Annabel, that there are times when I must be alone with no one but myself to think of and no sexual distractions.'

'I didn't think of myself as a sexual distraction in your life,' she said, but she didn't pursue the matter further. She guessed that his other marriages had failed because the women had been too possessive. She was determined that her marriage wouldn't fail in the same way.

'I'm sorry,' she said. 'I'll try to understand.'

That had seemed to touch him for he had been unusually tender for a while after that, holding her close and telling what a wise little girl she was.

'So many women want strings firmly attached,' he'd told her, 'and no man likes to live in bondage.'

Although this wasn't exactly what she wanted to hear, she told herself that, if she wanted to keep Joe, she would have to learn to be the kind of girl who could hold him, adjust to his moods and be there for him when he was ready for loving. He was a prestigious writer and she was lucky to be chosen to share his life.

It was two days after Joe had left for Glasgow when Annabel met Colonel Ramsay in the entrance hall of the flats. She had spent a depressing day with Jessie and had returned home hoping that Joe would telephone this evening.

Beyond passing the time of day and commenting on the weather, she hadn't had much contact with the other tenants of the flats since her party, but today Colonel Ramsay called out to her as she started up the stairs.

'I take it you've been out all day, Mrs Clifton.'

'Yes,' replied Annabel, a little surprised at his question. 'I've been visiting my sister.'

'So you missed the drama.'

'Drama?'

'Yes. That poor little lass in No. 6 tried to kill herself.'

'What?'

Annabel halted with one foot on the stair. 'What did you say?'

'Tracy Atkins. Tried to kill herself. Fortunately the window-cleaner was working here today and he saw her with her head in the gas oven. We managed to force the door and get her out in time.'

Annabel stood, shocked, unable at first to speak. Then she said, 'How terrible! Why did she do it? Is she all right?'

'Yes. We got her out in time. She's with her parents now. Nice people. Must have been worrying for them, a young, attractive girl living alone.'

Annabel was silent, shocked. The girl had always seemed hostile, rejecting any attempts at friendliness, but to try to kill herself, why?

'How dreadful,' she said. Then, for some reason she couldn't understand, she felt she had to justify herself to Colonel Ramsay.

'*I've* tried to be friendly towards her, but she rebuffs me every time.' She could have said 'In fact, she's downright hostile.' She looked appealingly at Colonel Ramsay. 'Is there anything we can do?'

He shook his head. 'No. I've given the parents my phone number and I've told them I'll keep an eye on the flat, gather up the post and keep it for them. I'm having the door repaired and I'm going to keep a key.'

'Oh dear,' said Annabel. If only Joe were here she thought. He'd know what to say.

'Well, if there's anything at all I can do,' she said, 'please let me know. As I said, I *have* tried to be friendly, but I got the impression she didn't want to mix.'

Colonel Ramsay smiled at her. 'Don't worry about it Mrs Clifton. It takes a clever person to understand the youngsters of today.'

But this girl is young, he thought, yet she seems more mature.

'Well, I'd better go in,' said Annabel. 'I've spent the day with my sister.'

'Oh, and how is Mrs Freeman? Better I hope?'

'Much better, thank you. Albert is a tower of strength.'

'Ah, he *would* be,' said the colonel. 'Such a devoted couple. Give them my best wishes when next you speak to them.'

'I certainly will,' said Annabel. 'Thank you.'

As she ran up the stairs she thought of the poor girl in No. 6. Man trouble probably. Oh, thank God I'm over that now. I've got Joe.

She let heself into the flat and prayed that tonight Joe would ring her.

The days and nights were bleak without him.

CHAPTER NINETEEN

Joe *did* ring that evening.

'Oh, you're in,' he said. 'I didn't expect to get a reply.'

'Of course I'm in,' she told him. 'I was hoping and praying that you'd call. I miss you so terribly.'

He was silent and she was afraid they'd been cut off, then he said, 'I don't want you staying in glued to the phone. Cultivate your social life, Annabel. Get out more. I'm sure Pepper Finlay could provide you with plenty of diversion.

You're too young to stay cooped up in that flat every evening.'

'I'm not cooped up, Joe. I'm just counting the hours and days until you come home again.'

'That's silly, Annabel. As for my coming home, I may have to stay longer here than I thought. I've struck a few problems.'

'Oh.' Her spirits drooped. 'I was so looking forward to your coming home on Friday.'

'Friday's impossible, sweetheart.'

'What sort of problems have you got?'

'None that you would understand, sweetheart.'

'You won't know until you try me.'

'Listen, Annabel,' he said. 'I have to go. I've got an appointment in half an hour and I haven't showered yet.'

'What sort of appointment? Not with a woman I hope.'

He was silent again and she was afraid she'd overstepped the mark. Then he said shortly, 'No. Not with a woman as it happens, although there *are* females in the publishing world, you know.'

'I know. I'm sorry, darling. I don't mean to be tedious. It's just that I was so looking forward to your return on Friday. When do you think you'll be back?'

'I don't know. I have things to sort out. I'll let you know in due course.'

'Oh dear,' she said, attempting flippancy. 'We do sound businesslike.'

'Annabel,' he said, 'I have to hang up or I'm going to be late for my appointment.'

'Oh, Joe darling, stay just another minute. Something awful happened here today. I almost forgot to tell you.'

Before he could reply she went on briefly to relate the story of Tracy Atkins' attemped suicide. 'Do you think I should try to get in touch with her parents, Joe, to see if there's anything I can do if and when she returns to the flat . . . ?'

He cut her short.

'Definitely not. They won't want *you* poking your nose in. It's nothing to do with you.'

'I was only trying to be neighbourly.'

'Leave it,' he said curtly. 'Just leave it. I must go, Annabel, I'll ring you again in a day or so. Goodbye.'

No farewell message of love. As she moved away from the phone depression swamped her. The evening ahead stretched empty, miserable. She thought of Jessie's remarks about living in the evil belt. Well, it was certainly true in the case of poor Tracy Atkins, but not for me Annabel tried to reassure herself. It hasn't been evil for me. It's given me Joe. She went into the kitchen to find something to eat for dinner, but she was disinclined to cook for herself. She felt restless and strangely depressed. On an impulse she rang Pepper.

'Could you find me a table for one for dins tonight? I've spent the day listening to Jessie telling me what a mess I'm making of my life and Joe's just phoned to say he won't be back on Friday after all and, to make things worse, we've had an attempted suicide here today.' And she proceeded to relate to Pepper the drama of Tracy Atkins. She finished up by saying, 'I just can't face a solitary meal here tonight. If you could find me a small table in a corner I'd be grateful.'

'I can do better than that,' Pepper said, 'David and I will be eating at eight. Come over and join us.'

'Are you sure, Pep? I don't want to butt in.'

'Butt in on what? We're just two hoteliers sampling our own fare. You'd be a welcome diversion.'

'It seems an awful nerve.'

'Listen, Annie, what are friends for? Oh God! How trite that sounds. I must be getting maudlin in my old age.'

Annabel arrived at the Crown in time to join pepper and David in the bar for pre-dinner cocktails. She told them about the lecture she'd received from Jessie and how she'd returned home to hear the shocking news about Tracy Atkins.

'Her parents are nice people,' David said. 'I know they've been worried about the girl leaving home to live in that flat and, to add to their worry, they firmly believe in the old saying—evil between the waters of the sea and canal.'

'Man trouble I expect,' said Annabel.

Pepper and David were silent, then Pepper said, 'I'm glad I'm not young any more.'

With a quick glance at Annabel's downcast face David said lightly, 'Aren't those the words of a song, Pep?'

'Yes.'

Pepper's eyes softened. 'Gigi, Maurice Chevalier—nostalgia.'

Annabel glanced at her quickly. She thought Pepper seemed a little distraite tonight, even sad. Tentatively she asked, 'Are you feeling all right, Pep?'

Pepper immediately switched on her smile. 'I'm fine, Annie. Why do you ask?'

'I thought .. well, I thought you seemed just then as if you were far away.'

'Oh, I get fanciful sometimes. I think it was mention of that song that sent me.'

'Pep really needs to get away,' David said. 'Her heart is way over the other side of the world.'

Annabel was intrigued. 'Why? What do you mean?'

Pepper picked up her glass and took a sip of her wine. The soft look had gone from her eyes.

'Oh, it's nothing, Annie. An old love has cropped up in Australia. He's in trouble, his wife has asked him for a divorce.'

'Oh,' said Annabel. 'Why has she done that? Has she found someone else?'

Pepper shrugged.

'Very likely, or it could be because Mark, her husband, is now confined to a wheelchair after a riding accident.'

'Oh, how awful! How terrible for him! And you want to go to him?'

Pepper grinned bleakly. 'Going to him was my first urge, Florence Nightingale reincarnated, but now I'm asking myself why the hell I should when he ditched me for her ages ago.'

Annabel was silent. She had known Pepper for years, but had never before heard about this man.

'And you'd go to him now?'

Pepper uttered a short laugh. 'Probably, if I were at a loose end and trying for Brownie points, but maybe it's a good thing I'm not. I have my commitments here with David and the Crown.'

'I keep telling her,' David said, 'that if she really wants to go I'll understand.'

'And leave you in the hands of some inefficient female to take my role and run this place into the ground.' Pepper laughed. 'No chance, David. I'd never do that to you and the Crown.'

Now that the conversation had taken on a lighter tone Annabel said, 'Well, if I were not going to marry Joe, I'd offer myself as David's business partner, although I know nothing about the running of an hotel, but I'd be willing to learn.'

'Well, it's all speculation,' said Pepper, brisk now, 'and never likely to happen, so let's order, shall we? I'm starving.'

Annabel's spirits rose during dinner as Pepper and David made light, laughing conversation. The man in Australia was not mentioned again. Annabel talked about when her divorce was finalized and she would be free to marry Joe.

'May I be your bridesmaid, Annie?' Pepper asked. 'Do you know, I've never been a bridesmaid. I always hated my cousin Julie because she was so pretty and was always being asked to be somebody's bridesmaid.'

'I was Jessie's bridesmaid,' said Annabel, 'and a right fusspot she was, told me I was not to flirt with Albert's best man. As if I would.'

'Who was Albert's best man?' asked David.

'Laurie Basset.'

Both Pepper and David giggled.

'But he's got adenoids,' said Pepper, '*and* he squints.'

'Shame on you Pep,' said David. '"Laugh ye not at the afflicted".'

'Is that a quote from the Bible?' asked Annabel.

'He wouldn't know,' said Pepper. 'I doubt if he's ever read the Bible.'

Annabel sighed. 'Time's going to drag until I'm free to marry Joe, but I guess I'll just have to be patient.'

Pepper caught the flash of dismay in David's

eyes and said quickly, 'Don't rush into another marriage, Annie. Enjoy your freedom while you can.'

Before Annabel could reply a waiter came over to the table and told David he was wanted on the phone. After he'd gone Annabel directed the conversation on to Jessie and Albert. For some reason she didn't want to discuss Joe with Pepper.

'Jess told me that some awful woman who cleans for Dora Hunter-Bell started a malicious rumour about Albert and one of his salesgirls.'

'Albert?' Pepper's eyebrows shot up. 'Albert Freeman? Never!'

'That's what I said, but I'm wondering if that's what caused Jessie's heart trouble.'

'*Oh*, I shouldn't think so. I'm sure Jessie knows she can trust Albert. After all, who'd want Albert and, anyway, I wouldn't think he'd know what to do.'

Annabel smiled faintly. 'Oh, I don't think Jess has any doubts now about Albert's fidelity, but you know how people gossip in small towns.'

'Yes,' said Pepper thoughtfully. 'I've never seen any assistant in Albert's store remotely like a *femme fatale*.'

Annabel giggled. 'And Albert's not exactly destiny's dream boy.'

David came back then and sat down at the table.

Pepper looked at him. 'Trouble?'

'No. Just a quote for a birthday dinner party.'

'We were just talking about Annabel's brother-in-law,' said Pepper, 'and a malicious rumour going round that he was having it off with one of his assistants.'

'Never,' said David. 'Not Albert Freeman. I'd accuse the pope before Albert.'

'That's what I think,' said Annabel and the subject of Albert's reputed indiscretion was dropped.

*   *   *

Three weeks passed and still Joe had not returned. He telephoned every two or three days with plausible excuses for not returning.

'You have to understand,' he told her, 'that my work takes me away sometimes for months, even years.'

After a while she settled into a routine, visiting Jessie regularly, going on window-shopping expeditions with Pepper and having coffee occasionally with Miranda Phillips, the resident of Flat 2 on the ground floor who went out of her way to be friendly. Joe Linden was never discussed between them; their conversation was mostly concerned with Jessie and Albert, great friends of Miranda. Jessie approved of her sister getting to know Miranda Phillips but Annabel laughingly told Jessie, 'I

181

can't forget that she's a headmistress and I feel I ought to put my hand up for permission to speak.'

'Such a good man your brother-in-law,' Miranda told Annabel. 'A man like Albert Freeman restores one's faith in decency, always reliable, always loyal to his wife and his religious upbringing. He's a good businessman too, polite, always calm.'

If she could have seen Albert Freeman on the morning Laura Collins's replacement, Brenda Hill, told Albert that she was collecting for a wedding present for Laura she would have seen a very different Albert. He fairly shouted at the poor woman.

'What on earth are you talking about?'

'Miss Collins, Mr Freeman.' She smiled coyly. 'Soon to be Mrs Meadows.'

She recoiled slightly in front of her employer. She had never seen Mr Freeman like this, even when a member of staff made a mistake. He was usually so calm and tolerant.

'Miss Collins is going to marry Mr Meadows,' she gushed. 'The man she went to work with when she left here so suddenly. I guess that's the reason she left after all those years; dark horse, eh, Mr Freeman?'

Albert tried to control his shock. Laura! My Laura! How could you?

'We thought we'd like to buy her a wedding present, Mr Freeman,' the woman continued eyeing him anxiously, 'and we thought you . . .'

'No,' he said harshly. 'No. I gave generously when she left here. She no longer has any connection with this business. I shall certainly make no further contribution. What you and the rest of the staff do is your own concern but I don't want the name of Freeman's to be connected with any wedding gift.'

And Albert went into his little office and slammed the door, something he had never done before.

In all her years at Freeman's Brenda Hill had never seen her employer in a mood like this. She put it down to the strain of his wife's illness. She would have to tell the rest of the staff how he had reacted to the suggestion of a wedding present and ask them not to tell Laura Collins about it when they saw her. Brenda was sure Laura would be hurt if she knew, she was such a gentle soul. Brenda thought of Laura's forthcoming happiness and sighed for herself and her own long engagement with no immediate prospect of marriage. Ah well, she said silently, at least Laura will no longer be living in the evil strip between the sea and canal and she'll have someone to help her with that cantankerous old mother of hers.

Alone in his office Albert sat with his bitter thoughts. God was certainly punishing him for his sins, firstly snatching love from him and now rubbing salt into the wound. And, at home, Jessie was getting more and more fretful every day. He pulled a ledger towards him and flipped over the pages. Takings were well up on last year. For that, at least, he supposed he should be thankful but Laura's fickleness lay like a heavy stone on his heart.

CHAPTER TWENTY

'Has that fancy man of yours returned yet?' asked Jessie.

'If you mean Joe,' said Annabel coldly, 'no, not yet. He has a lot of research to do.'

'So what happens when you're married to him? *If* you're ever married to him.'

'I shall respect his work and his need to be alone.'

'If he *is* alone.'

'Jessie,' Annabel said, 'I know you're sick and we're supposed to humour you, but I find your attitude most offensive. When you get to know Joe maybe you'll change your mind about him.'

'I can't see us getting to know him as you put it.' Jessie turned her head away. Her voice was weaker when she added, 'I'm sure he's not the kind of man Albert could ever be friends with.'

'If you mean he's not a mealy-mouthed church-goer,' Annabel said sharply, 'then, no, I can't see him and Albert ever being close friends, but at least they can behave in a civilized manner. After all, we shall be family and as neither you or I seem likely to have children, I think we should hang on to that. But, you never know,' she added thoughtfully. '*I'm* not too old for child-bearing. It's just possible that Joe might like a child. Yes . . .' Her eyes brightened. 'Yes, I guess he might at that. There's been no child from his other marriages, maybe I can give him something the other women couldn't.'

Jessie snorted.

'Let's wait and see what he gives *you* first. He doesn't seem in a hurry to get back to you. Has he given you a ring yet?'

'No. Not yet. Anyway, I don't want one.' Annabel rose and picked up her handbag. 'I'd better go, Jess. You seem determined to say horrid things about my future husband. I thought your attitude towards Alex was bad enough, but you're even more unkind about Joe.'

'I hear that Alex has gone to live in London,' said Jessie.

'Yes. I hope he finds happiness, but I think he's got a lot of growing up to do first.'

'His floozie has left the district too, I hear.'

'Well, you hear more than I do,' said Annabel frostily. 'I'm not interested in local gossip. I've been lucky enough to find happinesss and I thank God for that.'

She bent down to plant a fleeting kiss on Jessie's pale cheek, but Jessie caught at her hand.

'I'm sorry Annabel. I don't mean to be beastly to you, but I do worry about you so much and I know that Mumma would have wanted me to take care of you.'

Annabel relaxed and smiled at her sister.

'Boot's on the other foot though, Jess, isn't it? *You're* the one who needs looking after now. Are you sure you're feeling better? You look very pale today.'

Jessie smiled wanly. 'Yes. It'll take time. The doctor says I've got to rest a lot, but Albert is so good. He waits on me hand and foot and he's so patient when I snap at him, and I'm afraid I do, quite a lot. I try not to. I know he has worries at the store, but he doesn't say much about them to me for fear of distressing me.'

'I thought the store was flourishing,' said Annabel. 'It always seems to be busy.'

'Yes,' said Jessie. 'But it's the staff. That Miss Collins who was such a good worker and there for years has left to get married and although Brenda Hill is very conscientious, I don't think she's as capable as Miss Collins. Albert can't depend on her the way he used to with Miss Collins.'

'Well, bully for Miss Collins,' said Annabel, as she moved towards the door. 'But don't worry your head about it, Jess. Leave it to Albert. I'm sure he's well able to cope. All you have to do is to concentrate on getting well.'

Her heart was lighter as she drove away. Joe had said that he would probably be back by the weekend. Her divorce was proceeding smoothly and soon she would be Mrs Joe Linden, wife of one of the country's most prestigious authors.

She was surprised to see David Seymour's car parked in the forecourt of the flats when she got back to Romney Place. She put her car in the garage and went into the building. David was sitting on a seat on the ground floor of the flats. He rose when she entered.

'David! What brings you here?'

He took her arm. 'Let's go upstairs.'

She freed herself from his hold. 'David, what's wrong? Pep? Is she . . .?'

'No. Let's go upstairs, Annabel, please.'

Bewildered, she allowed him to take her arm and lead her up the short flight of stairs.

'Give me your key, Annabel.

Dumbly she handed it to him and he opened the door, standing back to let her enter.

'Sit down, Annabel, and I'll get us a drink.'

Puzzled, she shrugged out of her jacket and sat down on the settee.

'It's bad news, isn't it?'

'Yes. I'm afraid it is.'

'Is it Pepper? Is she . . .?'

'No, Annabel, it's not Pep. Is a brandy and soda all right?'

Without waiting for her reply, he poured the drink but, for himself, he poured only soda water. He turned and handed her the glass.

'Take a good sip of that, Annabel.'

Obediently she drank, her eyes beseeching him.

'Tell me, David. If it's not Pep, then who is it? Is it . . .?'

He pulled forward a chair and straddled it, putting his drink down on a small table, untouched.

'It's Joe Linden, Annabel.'

She started up. 'Joe. He's hurt . . .'

'No, Annabel, he's not hurt. Sit down, sweetheart. There's no easy way to tell you this. He's gone, Annabel, gone right out of your life.'

She put her glass down and stared at him, her eyes wide with disbelief.

'Gone? Where?'

'To Scotland with Tracy Atkins.'

She flung her hands out and knocked the glass of brandy to the floor.

'Tracy Atkins?'

'There was no easy way to tell you, Annabel.'

He longed to take her in his arms and cuddle her like he would a child, but he held himself in check whilst Annabel watched the brandy soak into the carpet as if mesmerized.

'The girl tried to kill herself because she was pregnant by him but it seems he's done the decent thing and accepted responsibility for her and the child.'

Annabel was staring at him as if he were crazy.

'I don't believe it.'

'It's true, dear.'

She was shaking her head from side to side like a crazy woman.

'He can't go. His flat . . .'

'Is rented, furnished.'

David reached over and took her hands in his.

'It seems they've been having an affair ever since he came to live in this building. I know her parents very well and they were aware of it and extremely worried about her. Then you came on the scene and they hoped she would accept that her affair with him was over, but when she discovered she was pregnant . . .'

'Stop it, David. Stop it.'

David rose, drawing her up with him. Then he held her in his arms.

'Cry if you want to, Annie. I have all the time in the world.'

He could feel her body heaving, but he knew the sobs were dry inside her, wrung from her broken heart. Presently he said, 'We want you to pack a small case and come over to the Crown for a day or two until you've got over the shock.'

She moved out of his embrace and stared at him with unseeing eyes.

'I don't need to go away, David, thank you all the same. I shall be quite all right here.' She gave a harsh laugh. 'They were right, weren't they, it *is* the evil belt?' She laughed again, this time a high-pitched sound, almost hysterical.

189

'What a ball Jess will have. "I told you so Annabel. Mumma would have told you . . ." Oh David, what a blind idiot I've been.'

Unresisting she allowed him to lead her back to the chair. He bent down and picked up her glass.

'I'd better mop up your carpet and get you another drink.'

She gave a brittle laugh.

'Don't bother with the carpet. I shall move away from here as soon as I can, but I *would* like another drink, a strong one.'

In spite of his pleas she refused to go to the Crown with him.

'Maybe Pep would call round this evening after dinner if she's not too busy,' she said. 'I'd like that.'

'I'm sure she will, but in the meantime . . .'

'In the meantime I shall be busy, David. I shall put this place on the market and work out where I want to go.' She laughed curtly. 'Somewhere away from the evil belt this time; in fact, right away from Copmarsh I think.'

'I hate leaving you like this, Annabel. What will you do for food?'

'Oh, I've plenty of food,' she said lightly, 'my freezer's stocked up ready for Joe's return. *And* I've plenty of booze.'

'Drink is not the solution, Annabel.'

'Oh, don't worry David. I won't let that bastard turn me into an alcoholic.'

'I can stay a while longer if you like,

Annabel.'

'No David. You have a hotel to run. It was good of you to come and tell me, instead of leaving me to find out for myself.' Again the bitter laugh. 'I presume Joe will ring me or write to say he's dumped me.'

'You promise to ring immediately, Annabel, if there's anything we can do, or if you find you can't cope.'

'I promise, David, and thank you.'

When he had gone she stayed in her chair and swallowed the fresh drink he'd poured her, then she went to the telephone and dialled Jessie's number.

'I thought you'd like to know Jess, your worries are over. Joe has dumped me for a young girl who lives in these flats.' Her voice rose a tone. 'She has a prior claim, see? Because she's pregnant by him.' Without waiting for her sister's reply, she added, 'I'm sure you and Albert will be delighted to know that Joe Linden is out of my life and not busting into our illustrious family.'

*   *   *

When Jessie got through to Albert he received her news with surprising calm.

'I'm glad she's come to her senses.'

'She hasn't, Albert. *He's* the one who's walked out. I'm worried about her. She was so calm about it, almost like a machine and she rang off before I could say anything.'

'Stop worrying, Jess, and be glad. I'm sure Annabel's a survivor. And now, if you don't mind, I've more important things to do than worry about your sister's love life. I have a store to run.'

Jessie wept as she replaced the phone. Albert's reaction wasn't what she had expected. For all his many kindnesses he had seemed very distrait lately. She wondered if business at the store was as good as he assured her it was. She rang the bell for Maisie Webb.

'My pills please, Maisie. I feel rather faint.'

As for Albert, he had just received a visit from the vicar on the subject of the forthcoming wedding of Laura Collins and Ivor Meadows. The vicar had told them he couldn't give them the full wedding service as Laura had been divorced, but he had agreed to give them a blessing and make it as near to the proper wedding ceremony as possible with a choir and servers for Holy Communion in all the ceremonial attire.

'I know you'll be there to support me, Albert, especially as Miss Collins was one of your most valued employees for such a long time.'

'Indeed I shan't be, Vicar,' Albert had said. 'Miss Collins let me down badly at my busiest time. She gave me very little notice and I don't feel I'd be in the right frame of mind to assist at her wedding service.'

As he sat in the office lost in a welter of bitterness, Albert thought of what Jess had just told him on the phone.

Ah well, he said silently, that affair was doomed from the start. Annabel has always been too impulsive for her own good.

He hoped that now she would settle down and keep out of the limelight until her wretched divorce was out of the way. He opened the small back window of his office which looked out on to a tiny yard. There were three wooden tubs in the yard in which Laura had planted crocus bulbs. In other years he had taken them for granted, in fact, hardly noticing them, but now their tight buds seemed to mock him. Soon they would be open in full flower proclaiming the fresh beauty of spring. Oh Laura, my Laura, how could you have forgotten so soon?

Albert turned away from the window as someone knocked and opened his office door. Brenda Hill stood there, twisting her hands together nervously.

'Mr Freeman. Mr Freeman, the phone hasn't been put through to your office since lunch and I took the call downstairs. It's Mrs Freeman, sir, the maid says can you come at once, she's sent for the doctor. Mr Freeman, sir, she's collapsed.'

Albert pushed the woman aside, picked up his briefcase and made for the stairs. Jessie had ousted Laura Collins and her crocuses from his mind and she had brought him abruptly back into the bleak cheerless realm of reality.

CHAPTER TWENTY-ONE

Annabel roused herself from the torpor of her bitter thoughts and looked at her friend. Pepper's glass of whisky and soda stood on the table beside her chair, untouched, which was unusual; it occurred to Annabel that Pepper was worried about something. Her usual glossy mask had slipped.

'Are you all right, Pep?'

'Yes. Why wouldn't I be?'

'Not still thinking about that man in Australia?'

'I think about him all the time, but what's the use? It's too late now. I was second best last time. I don't know if I could be second best again.'

Annabel thrust aside her own troubles.

'If you love him and he's free now, it can't be too late surely?'

Pepper gave a hard little laugh. 'And continue to be second best, always knowing he's still thinking of *her*?'

Annabel was silent. She didn't know what to say, then Pepper said, 'I had a child by him, but I knew he'd fallen out of love with me so I gave up the kid.'

Annabel was shocked. Cool, detached Pepper with a child.

'A baby, Pep? You had a baby?'

'Yes. Oh, it's fine. It's being brought up by a cousin of Mark's so *he* sees it occasionally—in the role of a generous, courtesy uncle I gather.'

'It? What?'

'A boy,' Pepper said softly, 'and I've never even seen a picture of him. I didn't want to.'

'And Mark's wife, doesn't she . . .?'

'I don't think she ever knew about him. She wasn't married to Mark then. I gave up the baby when he was a month old, kidding myself I was lucky to have got out before I made an even bigger fool of myself, hanging on to a man who had never really loved me, but would do his duty for the sake of the child. No thanks. I had more pride then. I thought I could ride it out alone, so I made what the books call a dignified exit.'

'And the boy would now be . . .?'

'Twelve years old and, I hear, very happy with his foster-parents.'

'Would you like to see him?'

'I don't know, but now his father wants to see *me*. His wife is about to ditch him and he's scared of having to cope alone with his handicap. He was always a coward over pain.' She uttered a harsh laugh. 'He needs a nurse who'll double up as a lover, I reckon. Mind you, he's a handsome devil, I reckon there could be plenty of takers.'

195

'And you still love the man, don't you, Pep?'

Pepper shrugged. 'I try not to think too much about him. I thought I'd succeeded, but then, when he was in trouble, he zoomed back into my life, the selfish bastard. He even telephoned me the other night.' She smiled wanly. 'You've no idea what the sound of his voice did to me.'

'Yes, I think I have,' said Annabel softly, remembering the sound of Joe's voice recently on the telephone when he'd tried to let her down gently. Each word of his had dropped like a stone into her heart.

'Enough about me and my benighted love life,' said Pepper, brisk now. 'What are *your* plans, Annie?'

Annabel sighed. 'I don't really know. I can't stay on in this building. I hate it here now, but I don't want to go too far away whilst Jess is so ill.'

'But I thought she was doing well?'

'They say she is, but she seems very sick to me. She used to have such energy, but now . . .' She stopped as the telephone intruded into the conversation.

'Excuse me, Pep, it's probably the estate agent.'

But it was not the estate agent: it was Albert. She spoke softly for a few minutes, then she returned to Pepper who, at last, was sipping her drink.

'That was Albert,' she said. 'It's Jess, Pep,

she's dead.'

*   *   *

Albert had little time to be alone. Business and church friends rallied round giving him almost round-the-clock support and what little comfort they could. At home Maisie Webb hovered over him like a fussy hen over a chick. He had convinced himself that Jessie's heart condition had been no fault of his and that his explanation of the time he'd spent with Laura Collins had no bearing on her sudden illness. No, he had kept his marriage vows and, therefore, his conscience was clear. Laura's successor, Brenda Hill, was proving a tower of strength. She assumed the role of private secretary, acknowledging for him the many letters of sympathy, organizing his time at the store so that no one intruded on him unduly. He found her co-operation a great comfort. Of course, she was nothing like Laura, but he was glad of that. Laura had been his magic, now he had no magic in his life, just reality. All he had left was the business. That would be his entire life from now on, that and the church.

He had received a trite little missive of sympathy from Laura and Brenda had sent a formal acknowledgment as she had in the case of the other sympathy messages. Laura's wedding took place the day before Jessie's funeral and, on the day of the funeral, Laura and her new husband were honeymooning in the south of France. That much Albert had heard from Brenda Hill and he tried to put it out of his mind. He told himself he had been lucky in his marriage. Jessie had been a good, faithful wife but, as he mused, the image of Laura blurred his vision—serene, loyal, loving Laura. Her quiet beauty he knew would remain in his heart for ever. He was ashamed now of his first reaction when Jessie had died. Now I am free, oh, if only you had waited, Laura, we could have been together, but even as these thoughts had crowded his mind, he had known it could never have been. How could he have demeaned himself by marrying an employee and so soon after his wife's death? His prestige in the town would have been irreparably damaged. No way could he have faced the vicar, fellow choirmen and members of the Chamber of Commerce. No, even by dying Jessie still held him in bondage and the small town of Copmarsh had him firmly in its respectable grip. He was born here, lived and honoured here; he would die, rich, alone, cheated of the thrill of romantic love, but he would retain his dignity and, as long as he lived, Freeman & Son would continue to be a prestigious feature of Copmarsh.

* * *

Annabel's flat was sold within a month of

putting it back on the market. She still hadn't decided where she wanted to live so, for the time being, she arranged to put her furniture in store and take a room at the Crown whilst she considered her options.

Her brother-in-law seemed to have no need of her assistance. His church and Chamber of Commerce friends were still rallying round him and the maid, Maisie Webb, brought her niece to live in and act as under-housekeeper and general dogsbody which arrangement suited Albert very well. He hadn't been too keen on the idea of living in the house with just Maisie Webb, although, he reflected grimly, there could hardly be any scandal in the situation.

As for Annabel, he had no wish to be seen to be too friendly with her. He knew that there was some gossip about her in the town. Miranda Phillips, who lived in Annabel's building, and who had been a good friend of Jessie's, had told him of the affair between Joe Linden and Tracy Atkins and how the girl's father had come to Joe Linden's flat to clear out his belongings which must have been painful for Annabel, Miranda said. 'I feel sorry for her.' But Albert had brushed aside her sympathy saying that Annabel had always been a rebel and it served her right.

'You'd never have thought she and my Jessie were sisters,' he told Miranda. 'Annabel was always headstrong and selfish. We did our utmost to stop her marrying that first husband

199

of hers but she wouldn't listen. She pays more heed to that woman who runs the Crown, Pepper Finlay. Stupid name for a woman, Pepper, and it distressed poor Jessie sorely when she heard about Annabel's involvement with that disreputable writer. I'm just thankful that her mother didn't live to see it.' He sighed. 'Jessie was so like her mother you know, a really good woman.'

Miranda Phillips listened and said nothing. She hadn't had a lot to do with Annabel since the girl had come to live at Romney Place, but she was rather sorry for her. She certainly didn't see her as the wanton Albert Freeman seemed to think she was.

'Well, I think I shall miss her,' she told Albert. 'I was just getting to know her, but I can understand her wish to leave. The flat hasn't exactly been lucky for her.'

'No. Well, Jessie told her it was unlucky to live between the sea and the canal,' said Albert.

'Then I must watch out, but I've lived here for many years and I've never suffered any ill effects,' Miranda Phillips said gently—neither have I experienced any ecstasy, she thought ruefully as she listened to Albert extolling his late wife's virtues.

*   *   *

When Annabel moved into the Crown she saw very little of David Seymour. When she did encounter him, he was always kind and polite, but he was usually involved with the business of the hotel and, in the evenings, he had his dinner served to him in his room. When Annabel commented on this to Pepper, Pepper replied that there was a lot of work to be done for the forthcoming season and that David worked whilst he ate. 'It's only on very special occasions that he comes out into the dining-room to eat.'

'And I'm not a special occasion.' Annabel smiled ruefully.

'No, you're not now,' said Pepper. 'You're just one of our residents and the staff are not encouraged to "frat" with the paying guests.'

Both women had laughed, but Annabel felt a sense of rejection. Maybe David was despising her for her foolishness in falling so quickly for Joe Linden following the break-up of her marriage. Even so, she valued his good opinion and she would have welcomed his steady common sense and friendship.

'I can't understand why there isn't a woman in David's life,' she said to Pepper. 'He's not old, he's *very* attractive and . . .'

'You think he's attractive do you?' queried Pepper quietly.

'Yes, of course he is. You must see it.'

Pepper shrugged. 'I guess I've got used to it. We were good for each other when we started this partnership, we each had problems and we respected each other's memories. You could say we've never looked back!'

'And you've never wanted more?'

Pepper looked at her sharply. 'No. Neither has he; that is, I don't think so, at least, not from me.'

'But you're not happy, Pep.'

Annabel was surprised at her sudden knowledge. She had been so wrapped up in her own misery that she hadn't had time to consider the feelings of her friends.

'What is happiness? Domesticity, kids, mortgages, commitments. Oh, I'm a very lucky woman. I'm a partner in a flourishing, interesting concern and I'm healthy. What more could I want?'

'I don't know. I just know that *I've* never been so unhappy in my whole life.'

'Still sobbing into your pillow over Linden?'

'No. Oddly enough I don't think so. That was rather like cutting my finger. Some ointment and a bandage and it's already healing. I just . . .'

'Just what?'

Annabel shook her head. 'I'm like a ship without a rudder and the sea is calm and dull.'

'So you're a sitting duck for a pirate?'

'No. Not any more.'

Pepper was silent a moment, then she said, 'Put it all behind you and look forward, Annie. You're young, attractive and not exactly hard up. I'd say you've got it made.'

'Oh Pep, I've made such a fool of myself. I

think I ought to go into hiding until I've got over the shame and then emerge as one of the town's do-gooders.' She gave a low chuckle. 'I might even help Albert at the church.'

'I hardly think Albert would appreciate that,' Pepper grimaced.

'No. Maybe not. Oh, Pep, what shall I do?'

'Sit tight, kiddo, weigh your options, enjoy the summer, swimming, coffee parties or you can always open a ye olde gift shoppe and write off your losses against income tax if you're too bored.'

Annabel gave a wintry smile. 'Sounds madly exciting.'

'Well, it's just an idea. My guess is that you won't be bored for long. Cheer up, sweetheart, some women would give their eye teeth for what you've got.'

'Yes, I suppose so,' said Annabel thoughtfully. 'You're a tonic, Pep, thanks.'

And, before long, there'll be another man, said Pepper silently, if there isn't already. Oh, Annie, you don't know how lucky you are.

Both women were silent for a while, then Pepper said, 'I wonder if you see many snakes when you live in Australia?' She shuddered. 'I hate snakes.'

Annabel looked at her steadily. 'There must be many compensations,' she said quietly, 'and I don't suppose you'd see many snakes.'

'I guess not,' said Pepper thoughtfully. 'No, I guess not.'

CHAPTER TWENTY-TWO

Annabel was surprised to receive a phone call from Albert.

'Annabel, I think we should meet. I need to discuss with you the disposal of Jessie's jewellery and clothes. She has some furs.'

'Did she not make a will, Albert?'

'No,' said Albert shortly.

'Well, in that case I think *you* should be the one to deal with it.'

'It's mostly a question of the jewellery,' said Albert stiffly, 'a lot of it came from your mother and it's very valuable.'

'Well, I have no claim on it,' said Annabel quickly.

'That's not the point, Annabel. It's only right that you should be involved in its disposal.'

'Well, if you think I can help, I'll be glad to meet you, Albert.'

'Could you come to the store, or would you prefer me to visit you at your hotel?'

Annabel wondered why Albert didn't suggest that she should visit his house.

'I don't mind, Albert. I could come to the store if it would be easier for you.'

'It would rather if it's not inconvenient for you. Would eleven o'clock tomorrow suit you?'

'Yes. I'll be there at eleven.'

She had been speaking on the public telephone booth behind the bar and, as she emerged, she came face to face with David. She was about to step aside and pass him as he seemed always to be busy these days, but he stopped her.

'Is anything wrong, Annabel?'

She grinned ruefully. 'A duty call from my sainted brother-in-law. He wants to discuss the disposal of my late sister's belongings.'

'Is it going to upset you, Annabel?'

'No. Just a bit unexpected that's all. I hadn't given a thought to Jessie's effects as they call them.'

David looked at her anxiously. 'Would you care to come into my office and have a coffee? You look a bit fazed as my mum used to say.'

'But you're so busy David. I don't want to take up your valuable time.' She smiled at him tremulously.

'I'm never too busy for you, Annabel. Come along in. I was just going to take my coffee break anyway.'

'Where's Pep?'

'I think she's gone shopping.'

As he ushered her into his office he added, 'I'm a bit worried about her. She seems very unsettled these days.'

Annabel sank down in the chair he pulled up for her.

'It's that man in Australia,' she said. 'Pep wants to go to him, but she's scared, scared of being hurt again.'

David picked up the phone and ordered the coffee before he answered her. He sat down in the chair opposite her.

'Yes I think you're right. Poor old Pep.'

'I think,' said Annabel, 'that Pep should grab some happiness if she can. She obviously loves the man and, who knows, it might just work this time if that other woman goes out of his life.'

The coffee arrived then and David waited until the waitress had departed before he spoke.

'So you think she should take a chance on love then, Annabel?'

'If it were me, I think *I* would.' She smiled ruefully. 'In my own case I've had two disasters.' She looked at him earnestly. 'Do you think *I* should call it a day, or might I hope for third time lucky?'

'You're still very young, Annabel.'

'Just lately I feel a hundred.'

David picked up the coffee pot. 'Black or white?'

'White please, a little cream.'

He passed the coffee cup to her, then he said, 'I think you should go for third time lucky. Have you decided what you want to do with your life?' His eyes darkened. 'I hope you won't decide to move away from Copmarsh.'

'No. I don't want to do that. Pep suggests I open an olde worlde gift shoppe.'

'I think that's an excellent idea.'

She grinned. 'Well, before I go into that, I have to visit Albert. I'm going to see him at the store tomorrow morning. It'll be the first time I've ever been invited into Albert's sanctum.'

David grinned back at her. 'I don't often go into the store, but the few times I've been in there and seen Albert enclosed in that miniature glass-sided office at the top of the stairs I've always thought he was like the German lookout in a prison camp, all he needed was a spy glass and a gun.'

Annabel giggled and David thought how absurdly young she sipped her coffee.

'This is lovely coffee.'

'Boss man's perks.'

'Getting back to Pep's problem,' she said. 'You know about her child, of course?'

'Yes. I know the whole sad story.'

'Were they in Australia when the child was born?'

'No. Pep's never been to Australia. Mark had this offer to work as a journalist for a leading newspaper out there. They were in England making plans to emigrate when this other woman came into his life. Pep faded out of the picture and Mark and his woman went out to Australia. The baby went too and was adopted by an Australian couple.'

'Poor old Pep. What a terrible time she must have had.'

'Pep's got guts,' David said, then he added, 'Just like I'm sure you have, Annabel.'

207

They sat in companionable silence a while and Annabel felt strangely at peace, then she said, 'David, do you suppose that if I offered to take over Pep's interest in this hotel instead of opening a gift shop, she *would* go to Australia?' She smiled faintly. 'That is, if *you* were agreeable, of course.'

'Taking over Pep's commitments here, Annabel, would be far more involved than opening a gift shop; it couldn't be tried for six months and then given up unless we could find a suitable successor quickly, which I doubt.'

'And you wouldn't want me as a partner, would you?' she said soberly. 'You wouldn't trust me . . .'

He interrupted her, 'I don't think you're quite ready yet to make big decisions like that, and,' he added heavily, 'I don't think I'm equipped to cope with the rejection if it came.'

'I don't take business commitments lightly, David.'

'But you've never had any, Annabel, have you?'

'Not yet, but that's not to say I couldn't make out. I'd be willing to start at the bottom and learn. I'd even do washing up.'

'I'm sure you would, but I'm not certain it would be the right solution.' He laughed.

'For whom?'

'For all of us. You're still in shock at the moment. You need time to sort yourself out.'

'I don't seem to be much good at that.'

'Exactly. Give yourself time to think, Annabel.'

'Is it a very exacting job then?'

'No. Please note I have my tongue in my cheek when I say it's not so much hard graft. Pep's part is more on the ornamental side, the social side if you like but, nevertheless, a serious commitment. Patrons like to see the same faces. Hotels which switch their staff frequently are not so popular. We get the same people here year after year and they greet us like old friends and we know they are grateful that nothing has changed. The same applies to our local casual trade. Establishments which are constantly changing staff are never as popular as the old and tried ones. Pep has a natural charm. She never gushes, but patrons always get the impression that she is really pleased to see them and has plenty of time to attend to any problems they may have, or even time for just pleasant chit-chat.'

'And you think I haven't got Pep's talents in that respect?'

'I didn't say that. I just think . . .'

Swiftly she interrupted him. 'It's OK, David. I understand that you have the profits of the hotel to consider rather than the whim of a bored, discarded female.'

He looked distressed.

'That's not it at all, Annabel. I'm sorry if I gave you that impression. I was merely pointing out to you all aspects of the job. As for the work

209

side of it, you can see for yourself, it doesn't involve much labour, except for some simple book-keeping. We have a girl who comes in to type our letters and Pep supervises the shopping and makes herself generally ornamental on the social side. I'm quite sure you would be adequate in all those respects; but it's you I'm thinking of, Annabel. I think maybe once the novelty wore off you'd get bored. It's not exactly an exciting life.'

'I'm not looking for excitement any more, just . . .' She gave a miserable smile.

'Just what, Annabel?'

She looked at him, her mouth trembling and he wanted to kiss her.

'Just someone to need me, give me something to do that's worth while . . . David, if I made a serious commitment to you, would you please take me on?'

He was silent a while and she thought he was wondering how to reject her request as gently as possible, then he said with a wry smile, 'And you'd no longer be living between the sea and canal, the evil belt, just looking out over the marshes. Who knows, you might even see the ghosts of the old smugglers.'

Her pathetic little smile tore at his heart.

'I don't want ghosts. I think I prefer the living, David. Will you just consider it, please?'

He reached out and took her hands in his.

'I hope to God I'm doing the right thing for both of us, but we'll give it a try then, Annabel, shall we?'

'If you're willing to trust me, David.'

'Yes. Maybe I am, but we must take it one step at a time though. We mustn't rush things, steady as we go.'

'I understand, David, and I'll abide by all your conditions.'

'Thank you.' He added the word 'darling' under his breath. 'And I'll be with you all the way. That sounds like Pep's car. Shall we go out together and tell her she can go to Australia?'

She released her hands from his grasp and stood up.

'That sounds like a wonderful idea, David. Thank you. You won't regret it I promise you.'

He put his arm casually round her shoulders as they went out to greet Pepper.

'Trust me, Annabel,' he said, 'we shall know when the time is right.'

She smiled up at him, tears starting in her eyes. She knew what he meant and she was grateful for his understanding. The spring sunshine struggled through the clouds. She lifted her head and took a deep breath as she went with David to greet Pepper.

'Happy now, Annabel?' he asked her.

She moved a little closer to him.

'I shall be,' she said. 'You see, David, I've always loved the marshes.'

We hope you have enjoyed this Large Print book. Other Chivers Press or G.K. Hall & Co. Large Print books are available at your library or directly from the publishers.

For more information about current and forthcoming titles, please call or write, without obligation, to:

Chivers Press Limited
Windsor Bridge Road
Bath BA2 3AX
England
Tel. (01225) 335336

OR

G.K. Hall & Co.
P.O. Box 159
Thorndike, Maine 04986
USA
Tel. (800) 223-2336

All our Large Print titles are designed for easy reading, and all our books are made to last.